Being together was never going to happen.

Not the way he imagined. And she'd be shocked that he ever thought of her romantically. In her world, they were friends and would never be more. Out of respect for Rey, it couldn't be.

"Listen, Lilianna, you need to get Sebastian and settle in. I've got this. You don't need to get wrapped up in my messy life."

With her chin down, she glared at him. "You listen to me. I'm not abandoning that boy any more than you are. And you, my friend, need my help whether you are willing to admit it or not. I know your normal plan of action is to tackle any problem alone. But you can't do that this time."

She had no idea how much truth she spoke. He needed her too much, and that wasn't good for either of them. If he was to be a man of honor and integrity like his father raised him to be, he'd make sure she was safe and far from him.

A seventh-generation Texan, **Jolene Navarro** fills her life with family, faith and life's beautiful messiness. She knows that as much as the world changes, people stay the same: vow-keepers and heartbreakers. Jolene married a vow-keeper who shows her holding hands never gets old. When not writing, Jolene teaches art to teens and hangs out with her own four almost-grown kids. Find Jolene on Facebook or her blog, jolenenavarrowriter.com.

Books by Jolene Navarro

Love Inspired

Cowboys of Diamondback Ranch

The Texan's Secret Daughter
The Texan's Surprise Return
The Texan's Promise
The Texan's Unexpected Holiday
The Texan's Truth

Lone Star Legacy

Texas Daddy
The Texan's Twins
Lone Star Christmas

Lone Star Holiday
Lone Star Hero
A Texas Christmas Wish
The Soldier's Surprise Family

Love Inspired Historical

Lone Star Bride

Visit the Author Profile page at Harlequin.com for more titles.

The Texan's Truth

Jolene Navarro

LOVE INSPIRED
INSPIRATIONAL ROMANCE

LOVE INSPIRED®
INSPIRATIONAL ROMANCE

Recycling programs
for this product may
not exist in your area.

ISBN-13: 978-1-335-48886-2

The Texan's Truth

Copyright © 2021 by Jolene Navarro

This edition published by arrangement with Harlequin Books S.A.

For questions and comments about the quality of this book,
please contact us at CustomerService@Harlequin.com.

Love Inspired
22 Adelaide St. West, 40th Floor
Toronto, Ontario M5H 4E3, Canada
www.Harlequin.com

Printed in U.S.A.

And ye shall know the truth,
and the truth shall make you free.
—*John* 8:32

This is dedicated to all our frontline warriors, in hospitals and on the streets.

Chapter One

The steady pounding of Bridges Espinoza's footsteps vibrated throughout his body. With each hard hit on the packed sand, the pain tried to win, but he pushed back. His shepherd mix, Big Mack, kept a steady pace with him, staying close to his right leg.

The dog loved running as much as he did. This was their first time since he'd been shot in the middle of a domestic dispute. His mother's worst nightmare had come true. As a police officer he'd been hit in the line of duty. Now he was back home in Port Del Mar recovering from a shotgun wound to the shoulder.

Gritting his teeth against the burn, he measured each breath as he forced oxygen into his lungs, increasing their capacity.

The beach was full of summer tourists, brightly colored canopies and umbrellas. Trucks and SUVs were lined up yards away from the waves, creating a continuous line of chrome and tires. The pesky phone vibrated for the third time in less than an hour. He didn't bother to check it. Either his mother or one of his sisters was calling. Being one of seven kids was fun most of the time, but his mother was the definition of *gallina clueca*. The English terms, *mother hen* or *momma bear*, were tame compared to his mother. And in less time than it had taken for the bullet to rip through his shoulder, his two older sisters were right next to her, demanding to know where he was and what he was doing.

Are you sleeping enough? Are you eating good food? You should be at Momma's house. Why did you leave? It was a barrage of the same questions every time. They always ended with a lecture and a list of reasons he should be recovering at home with her, under their loving care.

For the first six weeks after leaving the hospital, he had stayed with his mother. Now he was renting a cabin a few miles down the road. But being in Port Del Mar wasn't close enough for them.

They wanted to be in control of all his time. Which was why he was hiding out at the Diamondback Ranch. His old service buddy, Damian De La Rosa, had offered a cabin on the property, and he'd taken it. It was close without being too close.

He was thirty-one. He pushed into the run. A soldier since he was eighteen. His heart pounded in his ears, but it couldn't stop his sisters' voices.

They didn't care that he'd served as an officer in San Antonio's K-9 unit; they had no faith that he could take care of himself. One bullet wound in the shoulder and they fell back to treating him like a helpless child.

He leaned into the pain. He was stronger than the injury.

His mother told everyone who would listen that he had come so close to dying that he needed to be surrounded by *familia*.

Cramps pinched at his calves as sweat rolled from his

hairline down his face. He should have brought water but giving up was not an option. Denying the pain, he focused his gaze on the pier ahead. The throbbing in his shoulder screamed at him. He controlled his body.

"Tío Bridges!" In the blurry distance, a small form jumped up and down, waving at him.

He squinted against the sun. That couldn't be right. Now hallucinations were stalking him. Without a doubt, he needed water. He couldn't believe he had forgotten it in his truck. Rookie mistake. Not good. He checked his watch. He'd been running longer than planned.

"Tío!" The boy was now sprinting toward him. No doubt it was Sebastian, Eduardo and Lilianna's son. The familiar twist hit his gut. Eduardo had been more than his second cousin. He'd been his best friend since they were in diapers.

Why was his son here? Sebastian should be in San Antonio with his mother. When had Lilianna returned to his small corner of the world in Port Del Mar?

All the emotions he worked hard to conceal assaulted him. He didn't like surprises.

Bridges stopped. The muscles in his legs threatened to give out and take him down. He let go of Big Mack's leash and leaned over. Bracing his hands on his knees, he closed his eyes for a moment to slow his breathing and heart rate.

Bridges scanned the tourists for Sebastian's mother. Lilianna. His heart did its usual hitch at the first sight of her. The surprise left him unprepared to see her. Not that she had a clue as to his confused feelings about her.

The three of them had been inseparable first grade. Until she married Eduardo. The first girl Bridges had ever loved. Not that she knew that. And she never would.

All the unwelcome emotions would lead to only trouble. Teeth gritted, he made sure his heart and brain knew she was firmly in the friend zone. She had to be.

He'd lived with this reality for over half his life. Since their junior year when Eduardo had announced in the school cafeteria that he would marry Lilianna.

The three of them had been hanging out and going on backyard adventures since first grade. He had always faced the world with a confidence Bridges struggled with. He preferred to analyze, plan and take it one step at a time, then revise when needed.

But Lilianna Perez Espinoza was here on his beach; there was no time for any of that. They weren't kids anymore. She was Eduardo's wife…his war widow. His heart twisted at their loss.

Her face was hidden under an oversize floppy straw hat. Her golden-brown skin glowed against the form-fitted orange tank top and flowing long skirt. It had a specific name, but he was clueless. His sisters would be rolling their eyes.

All he knew was that it looked good on her. He couldn't remember the last time he'd seen her in anything but scrubs.

At the funeral. Pain not related to his gunshot wound pulled at his chest. Eduardo Espinoza had been twenty-eight when they buried him. Lilianna's husband. Sebastian's dad.

Yes. That's what he needed to remember. He closed his eyes against the sight of her to give his mind a chance to get on board with his plan to see her as nothing more than a friend.

The small body crashed into him, and he instinctively pulled the boy closer. Was he imagining it, or had Sebastian lost weight? He was already small for his age; why would he be getting smaller? He took a breath and made eye contact with Lilianna. "What are y'all doing in Port Del Mar?" They'd both grown up here, but she hadn't been back since they'd moved her dad to San Antonio.

A gust of wind threatened to take her hat. One hand on the crown, she glanced sideways, a distressed look on her face. The expression disappeared quickly, but he saw it.

She changed her look to a hard glare and waved her free hand at him. "What are you doing?"

"Me?" He tried for the wide-eyed, innocent look, but they both knew she had caught him. She was a nurse and aware of his injuries. He shouldn't be working out this hard yet. "Just doing some R & R. The doctor said it would be good for me."

"I'm pretty sure he was thinking more along the lines of recovery and rehab or relaxing and resting. Walking, yes. Not running. Hard. On the beach. It can't be good for your injuries. Do you have water? Are you trying to kill yourself?"

Now she was sounding like his mother and sisters. The tiny arms moved into a death grip around him, followed by a low sob. Going down to his haunches, he shifted his shoulders to look the boy in the face. The normally healthy brown skin was pale, and his eyes looked too big for his face. Now Sebastian was crying. "Hey, Champ. What's wrong?"

"I thought you were dead. You didn't come back. Are you going to die?" His voice was so low, it was difficult to hear over the waves and wind. The narrow chest lurched with a hiccup.

Concerned, he looked up at Lilianna as he pulled the boy back into his arms. "I'm okay."

Lillianna was on her knees next to them. "Oh, sweetheart. I told you he was good. He needed time away to heal. I'm just being bossy like I get when people are sick."

His amber eyes went wide. "Abuelito got sick, and he died. And my daddy was hurt at work and never came home." He looked up at Bridges. "You haven't come to visit since Christmas. That was a long time ago. When I asked, Mom said you got hurt on the job. I waited for you."

His gaze shot up to Lilianna. "Why didn't you call me?" He took a deep breath at the thought of not being there when they needed him.

She rested a hand on her son's back, and her face softened. "Oh, sweetheart. Why didn't you tell me you were worried? We could have called him." She favored him with a smile, but it didn't reach her eyes.

He should have known the boy would miss the rides in his dad's truck. At least once a month, he managed to spend time in San Antonio to let Sebastian ride around in El Toro, Eduardo's beloved pickup. He had wanted to find a way to keep his cousin real for the son who had been too young to really remember him. "I'm sorry. With everything—"

"No apologies." She cut him off. "You've had enough to worry about. Your mom called me. She's concerned that you're doing too much, now that you aren't staying with her." She tried to smile again. It was brighter this time.

"They're not fans of mine right now." More like his mother and sisters were fuming mad with him for leaving. He was used to living on his own and needed his space, but they thought one of them should be by his side 24/7. "I stayed with her for six weeks after being released from the hospital." He didn't bother to add that he hadn't been able to breathe. And it had had nothing to do with his wound.

He soothed Sebastian's hair back. "I'm getting stronger every day, Champ." He flexed his good arm.

"Baby boy, Bridges is going to be fine." Her large brown eyes bored into him again. "Do you have water?"

"I hadn't planned to run this far." It had felt so good to be out. He had pushed his body a bit further than was safe, but there was no reason for her to know the details. "The water's in my truck, by the pier." He pointed behind her. "Mack and I were going in to get a drink. Really, it's not as bad as it looks." He stroked the wind-blown hair of the seven-year-old, who had Eduardo's eyes. He looked so much like his daddy. "You're good? Having fun is required when you're on a beach."

The boy mumbled a yes. Bridges looked to Lilianna for confirmation.

She nodded. "I would have called if I'd needed you. I promise."

He hadn't been needed. That was a blessing. It was. The pouting toddler inside him needed to grow up.

Seeking a distraction, he scanned the area. The beach was full of summer tourists, more than he had expected this early in the morning. "What brings you to the sunny beaches of Port Del Mar?"

Another gust of wind came up behind him, stronger than the last. Umbrellas flew overhead. He ducked and covered Sebastian. Debris flew over them, and Lilianna lost her grip on her straw hat. He started to go after it, but she stopped him. "Stay with Sebastian."

She ran after it. A woman they had gone to school with caught it. Lilianna spoke with her for a bit, then bent down and looked at her daughter. Then she pulled a small first-aid kit from her bag and did something with the girl's hand.

"What's Momma doing?"

"What she's good at. Helping others."

What was she doing here? Time off was a foreign concept for her. She hadn't taken any vacation since Eduardo's death three years ago. She was head nurse at one of the busiest emergency rooms in San Antonio.

"Is that little girl okay?" Sebastian asked him.

"They're all smiling, so I'm sure she is." He stroked the boy's hair. "Your mom's superpower is taking care of people."

"But mommy couldn't save Abuelito." He dug deeper into Bridges's neck. "Or my daddy."

Guilt hit him hard. He hadn't thought about how his being shot would affect the little guy.

Hooking his finger under the small chin, he made sure they had eye contact. "We don't always know why things happen, but your mom is not going anywhere. I'm always here for both of you. We just have to trust that God has it all under control, no matter what happens." He smiled, hoping he gave the boy a sense of peace he couldn't find for himself. If he could live by his own words, life would be easier.

With a hug and a wave, Lilianna walked back to them, her thick hair now flying free. The sun highlighted the red streaks hidden in the brown. With a grunt, he managed to steer his gaze to the waves. He should not be noticing the color of her hair.

Standing, he picked Sebastian up.

"Hey. Have you been to the beach before?"

"No. Momma said it was time for a vacation. She grew up here. With you and Daddy, right?"

"Yep. Our families hung out all the time." Once she married Eduardo, they never came back. Even when he came to visit. Why had she shown up without any warning? His mother should have known. She knew everything about the comings and goings of the small coastal town.

Standing in front of Bridges and her son, Lilianna pulled out two bottles of water from her bag.

"You have a full survival kit in that tote of yours." He winked.

Tilting her head, she narrowed her gaze. Was he trying to distract her? "You, sir, should not be holding him." Trading one of the waters for her son, she took a moment to hug him tight. He wriggled against the confinement, so she let him slip to the sand.

Bridges was letting his dog drink out of his bottle. Sebastian laughed, then he went to Bridges's dog and shared his water too.

"Sebastian. That's your water." She took the bottle and wiped the rim.

Narrowing her eyes, she glared at Bridges. "Dehydration is the number-one cause for accidents on the beach. You're pushing yourself too hard. What's going on? This is not like you."

Bridges grinned around the bottle as he took a long drink. He had the audacity to act like she was being childish. Lowering his water, he winked. "Nurse Lili-anna taking care of everyone. You can't stop yourself, can you? Just so you know, my mother and sisters are pushing me to my limits."

Bridges gave the dog the rest of his water, then walked toward the pier. Big Mack and Sebastian fol-lowed him. It had always been that way growing up. Ed-uardo had been louder and more outgoing, but Bridges had been their true leader. Strong, steady and silent— and always knowing which direction to take.

Unlike her husband who tended to charge into life at full throttle, Bridges naturally faded into the back-ground. Eduardo had loved his nickname, El Toro. Had even named that stupid truck The Bull. She bit back the sudden tears.

She knew Bridges had to miss Eduardo as much as she did, but he never talked about it. Was it hard for him to be around her and Sebastian? Was that the real rea-son he hadn't called or visited in the last five months?

She fell into step on the other side of him. "Has the doctor already released you to return to a full workout and lifting over fifteen pounds?"

He didn't bother to answer. They both knew the truth. She just wanted to hear him say it. Sebastian held the leash, although she knew that it was more to make peo-ple feel comfortable around the big dog. He wouldn't make a move without Bridges's permission.

She glanced back up at him. He was watching her with that crooked grin and a spark in his eyes.

"Don't you dare give me that look. You're not out of trouble."

"I thought you were on vacation. Shouldn't you take a break from saving lost causes?"

"You're not a lost cause. I'm just worried about you, and so is your family."

His good humor slipped right off his face. Shoving his hands in the pockets of his jogging shorts, he turned all his attention to staring at some unknown point in the distance. "Why are you and Sebastian here in Port Del Mar?"

"Like you said, vacation." That sounded weak to her own ears.

"When was the last time you took more than one or two days off work?"

"That's part of the problem. I haven't." She glanced at her son. He was happily chatting with the dog. "Sebastian hasn't been doing well. There have been bursts of angry fits that are not normal for him. He hasn't been eating. I need to spend more time with him. He's been acting out. The end of school wasn't easy. With all the financial responsibility being on my shoulders now, I worry about…" She rubbed her arm.

Sebastian looked over at her. "Are you okay, Momma?"

"Yes, sweetheart. Thank you. It's been an exciting morning. I'm ready to show you Tito's house and take a nap."

"A nap?" He didn't look happy about that, but he didn't say anything else. "Can I put my feet in the waves before we leave?"

She sighed, unsure. Bridges leaned a little forward. "Mack loves playing at the edge of the waves."

"Okay."

He cheered and jumped. With the dog right next to him, he dashed to the water's edge.

"Sebastian! Make sure you can see me. Stay with us. Do you understand?"

"Yes!" They were already in the water. The dog pounced on the waves and bit at the foam. Sebastian laughed. The sound warmed her heart and relaxed her. It had been a while since she'd heard true laughter from her son. It had also been too long since she'd heard it from the man walking next to her.

Eduardo, Bridges and her. The three of them had been inseparable all through school. Then the guys had joined the Army together. Leaving her out of their adventures for the first time.

But since Eduardo's death three years ago and especially over the last twelve months, Bridges had put distance between them. A distance she didn't understand. It was as if she had lost her husband and was now slowly losing her friend. She still had his family. They came to San Antonio often and always came by for a visit. She knew the feeling of isolation wasn't real, but she longed to be connected to family. And Port Del Mar was where she had the best memories.

She needed to find that again.

"I'm also here because I…" Too personal. "Sebastian was worried about you. It was a good time for both of us. He could use a dose of his favorite uncle. He also needed to see for himself that you're alive and healthy."

"You could have called. What's going on with him?"

"With my dad's death three months ago, I think Sebastian finally understands what it means when someone is dead. We were used to Eduardo being gone for long stretches of time with his deployments, and Bastian was only four. I'm not sure how many real memories he has of his father, but I think he's realizing he'll never see his dad again. Then you were shot. They had a Dads-and-Donuts thing in the last month of school. My dad had gone once before. You went last year. This one slipped past me. He had a meltdown." She sighed. The guilt at the thought of what Sebastian was going through stung her eyes with tears. "He doesn't know how to deal with all the uncertainty. I realized that spending so much time at work was how I was dealing with my grief. I can control the chaos in the Emergency room but not in my son's life."

She wrapped her arms around her middle and stopped to watch Sebastian playing in the waves with Bridges's dog. "My son needs me. And I need to get right with God. The ocean is a good place for that, so I took a leave of absence."

"I'm so sorry. I didn't even think about how my injury would affect him."

"It's okay. How could you? He's my responsibility and I need to make sure he's growing strong—physically, emotionally and spiritually." Her gaze stayed on Sebastian as he ran with the big dog. "He's growing so fast—and if I'm not careful, I'll miss it."

"Is he really okay?"

"Yes. Better than you." She gave him the look that told him she knew he was trying to get away with being told what to do.

"So, my mom called you?"

She laid her hand over her heart. "And your sisters." She laughed at the distress on his face. "Your mom is the one who suggested I come back. She thought I might have more influence over you. I'm supposed to tell you to go home."

He chuckled and watched the duo play in the waves.

"Where are you staying? I thought your dad's house was a vacation rental now."

"It was. There were a few bookings the manager had to find a new location for, but by 1:00 p.m., the cleaning crew should be done, and then it's all mine." She looked at her watch.

Bridges stopped at the edge of the pier. "Where are you parked?"

She pointed to the south end of the public parking lot. That's when she saw the truck. Her heart flipped and her throat tightened for a moment. The oversize black King Ranch Silverado was at the north edge, next to a tall sand dune. It had been Eduardo's pride and joy.

Whenever he returned from his deployments, he wanted to see Sebastian and her and then his truck, in that order. He'd get in and just drive them around for a few hours. She hadn't sat in the truck since the last time he'd come home.

After his death, she knew she had to sell it, but unable to let it go, she'd let the truck sit in the garage, unused. Finally, Bridges had offered to buy it. She loved the idea of him having it.

"Sebastian. Let's go." With her son in hand they walked to the cars.

"That's my Daddy's truck!" Sebastian jumped up and down. "I want to ride in it! Please. Please let me ride in it." That had been one of the best benefits. Bridges had made sure to take Sebastian out for rides, like Eduardo had done.

Lilianna sighed and tried to take his hand, but her son wiggled away and tried to dart across the parking lot. "Sebastian!"

Bridges stepped in front of the little runaway and

went to pick him up…again. She got there first and dropped to her haunches as she pulled her son to her. "Running across the parking lot is dangerous. We're going in our car."

He doubled up his little fist and lashed out in rage. "No! I want to ride in Daddy's truck. Let me go!"

"Stop." Her voice firm, she trapped his hand against her chest. Her baby boy was hurting and didn't understand his own rage. As his mom, it was her job to help him through these emotions he didn't understand. And she seemed to be failing.

She sighed and laid her head against his. Locking down the sobs tearing at her heart wasn't easy. She hadn't been doing a very good job of it this last year. "I'm sure if you ask nicely, Bridges will take you for a ride in his truck later. It's Tío Bridges's truck now."

Bridges knelt beside them. "Hey, Champ. That's not how you treat your mom. And you never hit a woman, no matter how angry you are. You need to apologize and not ever do that again."

Lilianna gritted her teeth. She knew he was helping, but it just made her feel even worse that Sebastian's arms relaxed under her grip at his words.

Face wet from tears, he wrapped his skinny arms around her neck. "I'm sorry, Momma."

She was so raw right now that she was teetering on the edge of a breakdown. No one needed to see that. She could not, would not do that in front of Bridges and Sebastian. They needed the strong woman who held everything together. When she found time to step into the shower, then her guard could drop.

Bridges pointed to her silver sedan. "Come on. Your

mom's car is over there, right?" He held out his hand, and her son skipped out of her arms to grab it.

Then he turned his now smiling face to her and slipped his free hand into hers. The anger vanished just as fast as it had flared. "I can go in my dad's truck later today?"

Her gut burned. After losing Eduardo and then her father, Sebastian had seemed to be doing so well, even thriving, but these last two months had ripped the bandage off the wound that had been hidden. They were going to have to find a way to heal it before there was permanent damage.

Her husband was gone. It seemed to have taken three years and the death of her father for Sebastian to truly understand what that meant. Maybe she had been stuck in denial too. With the job she had, it was easy to push it all down and ignore it.

Helping her son into the back seat, she took a deep breath to steady her nerves. She was in the long haul alone. This was just the beginning of her new journey.

Chapter Two

Sweat beaded on her forehead as heat burned under her skin. She glanced at the clock. Only one minute had passed. Why did it feel like an eternity since she had given Bridges a little wave goodbye?

He had stepped back, waiting for her to leave—and he was still standing there. She couldn't look his way. She turned the key again. A horrible weak *clank* came from her car. One deep breath, a pause and then another turn. Nothing.

She fell forward, her head thumping against the top of the steering wheel.

No. No. No. Why is this happening? Positive thoughts. She blew a long stream of air out until her lungs were empty. *The engine is going to start.* She filled her lungs and held her breath, counted to five then turned the key. *Nothing.*

A tapping sound brought her head up. Bridges stood there, probably wondering what she was doing. She lowered the window.

His hands braced on the top of her door, he leaned

down to look in the car. "Is it just me, or is your car not starting?"

Not gonna cry. I'm not gonna cry. "It's not starting." She forced a smile. "Hopefully, I just need a jump. I have charging cables in my trunk."

He helped her get the cables connected, with her portable battery jump starter. After waiting a while the engine still didn't turn over. She sighed. "I should just get it towed to a garage. Do you know of one I can trust? Does Solis still have his?"

"I'm not sure. Let me call Damian. Do you remember him?"

"De La Rosa? He went into the service after high school?"

"Yep. I'm staying in his old cabin on their ranch." After a few minutes, he hung up, then made another call. He smiled at her. "Yes. Solis is still in town. The tow truck will be here in fifteen."

"I could have—"

"Yes. You are more than capable of taking care of yourself and Sebastian, but it feels good to be here for you." He shoved his hands in his pockets and stared at the horizon. "Most of the time I just feel helpless."

"Thank you, Bridges." He had lost as much as she had, and he was now dealing with a shotgun wound. Something like that didn't just inflict physical damage. It took a mental toll, as well. She took a deep breath and released her frustration in the exhale. Getting upset wouldn't make anything better.

His need to help them was probably as strong as her need for independence. "Car trouble always sucks the joy out of a beautiful day. On the bright side, because you were ignoring the doctor's orders and running on the beach, I have someone I trust to help. You know how much I hate asking for aid. Thanks for giving us a lift."

Sebastian jumped out of the back seat and darted toward the big black truck. Bridges reached out and grabbed the escape artist before he ran past the car's trunk. His other hand went to his chest as pain flashed across his face.

She wasn't sure who she was more upset with. "Sebastian, what did I just tell you about running without looking?" She knelt in front of her son. "You hurt Tío Bridges."

The boy's big eyes flew to his hero. "I hurt you?"

He closed his eyes and rubbed his chest. "Just a little, but it's okay."

"It's not okay." She snapped.

Bridges twisted his face and gave her an apologetic grimace. "She's right. Moms always are." He pointed a finger at her. "But don't be telling my mother I said that." His full attention went back to Sebastian. "Listen. Darting through a parking lot is dangerous. Wait for your mother. You scared her. Scaring the people we love is not cool."

The tears filled her son's eyes. "I'm sorry, Momma." He took her hand. "I was excited."

"Stop and think before you rush into something and get hurt. And your Tío Bridges is still healing from his wounds, so we have to be careful with him."

She almost laughed at Bridges's indignant sound as he directed a hard glare her way. "I'm not that fragile. Come on. El Toro is waiting." He moved to the truck, Mack on his heels.

She rolled her eyes at the ridiculous name her husband had given his truck. He had loved his nickname and had christened everything in his life with it. He had even suggested it when they were expecting Sebastian. That had been a firm no. "Your dad and Tío Bridges spent a lot of time in this truck."

As Bridges helped Sebastian into the truck, she laid her hand on the cold, shiny metal. It was just a truck. She closed her eyes and imagined being somewhere else. With a deep breath, she joined them in the truck.

The scent and feel of the truck flooded her mind and brought on a wave of memories. She blinked back the tears that burned her eyes. She was over this. She was.

"Are you my real uncle?" Sebastian asked, as Bridges snapped the seat belt in place. The dog lay down and rested his nose on her son's leg. "Angie says you're hers, so I can't call you uncle. What's a second cousin?"

"Our grandfathers were brothers." Bridges's oldest niece was eleven and liked telling people what to do. Just like her mother and grandmother. To say that the women in Bridges's family were strong-willed would be an understatement. Marguerite, Angie's mother, was the oldest Espinoza sibling—and probably the biggest reason Bridges was avoiding his family.

The masculine laughter filled the truck's cab. "She's like her mom and tells people what to do when she doesn't even know what she's talking about. I'm your uncle because your father and I were cousins and best friends when we were still in diapers. Your mom joined us in first grade. We are closer to each other than to our brothers and sisters. So, you'll continue to call me *tío*, because that's what your father wanted."

"Did my father like first grade?"

"School was not your father's favorite place." He

winked and smiled in the rearview mirror. "I can tell you a million stories about your dad."

She glared at him, silently warning him to proceed with caution. This was the problem of growing up with someone. They knew your childhood secrets. There was no pretending or starting over with a clean slate. She also knew that this was one of the reasons she was here. Her son needed to talk about his father, and Bridges knew him better than anyone.

"Your dad and first grade?" He pressed his lips together and glanced up, like he was giving it a lot of thought. "He loved being outdoors, but there were a few classes that made him excited to go to school. He liked science, but he lived for PE and recess."

"Me too. I'm just like him."

Lilianna sighed. "Yes, you are a lot like him, but you love reading your books too. And making mazes." She looked to Bridges. "You should see his latest drawings. They're incredible."

"Books are lame." He crossed his arms over his chest and pouted.

"Mazes? Those take a lot of planning and navigational skills." Bridges jumped in, pretending not to hear the last sentence. "That sounds cool. You'll have to show me. Your dad wasn't very patient with sitting still. He spent a lot of time trying to get me and your mom to do his homework. If he'd just done it without the fuss, it would have saved him a ton of time. One of the reasons we called him El Toro was because of his tendency to charge into things."

Charging in without thought was left unsaid. Which was probably a good thing right now.

The faded memories came back full force, and she couldn't hold back the laughter. "That is so true."

Sebastian leaned forward. "Did he get in a lot of trouble?"

Bridges glanced at Lilianna before twisting to look at the mini version of Eduardo. She didn't want to lie to her son, but she also wanted him to develop a love for school. Eduardo had hated sitting at a desk. "How do you measure *a lot*?"

She shook her head. Thinking of Eduardo wasn't as painful when she was with Bridges.

Was this where she and Sebastian needed to be right now? She'd left this town as fast as she could. She had loved living in the city, but it was starting to feel too big. She was so tired of being strong and alone. Maybe she was ignoring what God really wanted her to do. Twisting around, she studied her son. Coming home felt right. But was she here to stay for good, or just for the summer?

Bridges took his time and picked his words carefully. Lilianna had given him a clear message that whatever he said about Eduardo would have a powerful impact on Sebastian.

In the rearview mirror, he studied the small boy. He looked so much like his father that it hurt Bridges's chest. There had been such fury in those little fists earlier. Sebastian had never been one to throw fits, even as a toddler. He'd always been an easygoing kid.

To reassure her, he winked, then continued. "Once he found a tarantula on the way to school and decided to keep it. Mrs. Peterson was not happy when he pulled it out of the paper bag, and most of the girls screamed. Except for your mom. She had her hands on her hips and told him to free it so we could get back to math. Has she told you how much she loves math? And rules. She adores rules."

The little boy wrinkled his nose. "She has a lot of them. I like being outside. I don't like school and I don't want to go back."

Nervous, Bridges glanced at Lilianna, trying to let her know he was working hard to say the right things. "Rules keep us safe. I have great memories of your dad in school. It can be a good place to go and hang out with friends—"

"I don't want to go to school." He pulled into himself.

That twisted his heart. He shot Lilianna a concerned look. Every mother wanted to know that her child was happy. He was out of his element. "There's a cool store in town with all sorts of supplies and beach toys. Do you have any?" What kid wouldn't be happy with new toys?

"No," Sebastian mumbled from the back seat. Mack gave an encouraging bark. Turning to the big dog, the boy broke into the beginnings of a smile. "Big Mack and I want to build a sandcastle and ride waves."

"Buckets, shovels and boogie boards it is. I haven't been on one in ages."

"And you're not going on one anytime soon, Officer Espinoza." She gave him that look she used with her most stubborn patients. He wasn't going to win that battle.

"Port Del Mar Livery and Mercantile has everything we'd need. Maybe fishing poles would be good. Have any?"

"No. I want to go fishing. Can we go out on the big boats we saw at the pier?"

"Yep. My friend's family owns the charter company,

Saltwater Cowboys. The De La Rosas knew your dad too. You're going to meet a lot of people that can tell you all sorts of stories about him."

Lilianna made a face. "Maybe we should go back to San Antonio."

He laughed. "Chicken."

She rolled her eyes.

Driving down the main drag, he stopped in front of a strip of buildings that looked straight out of an old Western movie. "This store has been here for over a hundred years. It doesn't have horses anymore, but it has everything else. First stop, beach and fishing supplies. You up for some exploring and shopping?"

On the sidewalk, Sebastian held Mack's harness and waited at the door for them. Bridges could tell Lilianna was worried. "I've got this. Let me play uncle, okay? He deserves to be a little spoiled. It's not going to hurt anyone. We'll check on your car, then head to your dad's house. This might end up being a very good day, despite all the early indications."

"When did you become Mr. Sunshine?"

No reason to tell her it was all an act. He'd do anything to see her smile. Over the years, it was the motivation that had kept him going. If she was happy, that was all he needed. Standing next to Eduardo as his best man, he had endured their wedding day as one of the hardest in his life but watching her laugh and dance had made it worth it.

Right now, her smile was bright for Sebastian. In the old-fashioned store with the wood floors and glass cases, they gathered items that would make for a fun time on the beach and in the water. After walking next door, they grabbed some basic food supplies. As he was paying, Solis called. Her car just needed a new belt. It would be done by the end of the day.

Groceries loaded, she sighed and grinned at him. "You were so right. We already got to spend time on the beach and explore the old store. And we hung out with you. The day is beautiful." Playing with the edge of her skirt, she kept her head down. "A summer in Port Del Mar is a good plan for Sebastian and me."

"The summer?" He dropped the bag in the bed of the truck. "I thought it was for a couple of weeks. Aren't vacations usually like two weeks?"

She shrugged and glanced at his back seat, where Sebastian was talking to Mack. "I need real time with him. It's too tempting to go in to work whenever I'm called. So I'm off work for two months."

Two months. With her living next to his mom, he was going to be seeing a lot of Lilianna for two months. He let the silence sit between them as his mind and heart wrapped around that fact.

This was the reason he lived in Oklahoma. Close enough in an emergency, but far enough for him to stay sane.

Chapter Three

Before they pulled back into the street, her phone emitted a jazzy ring. When she picked it up, he saw his mother's name.

They made eye contact. She bit her lip and looked at him, then glanced away.

"Aren't you going to get that?" he asked, stifling a smile. He wasn't the only one afraid of his mother.

Her gaze went to the roof, then with a sigh, she lifted the phone to her ear. She greeted his mother in Spanish and told her that she had some car issues, but that it was all good.

On the other end, he heard his name. He knew he'd be wanted on the cell soon, so he pulled over and parked the truck. Lilianna shifted away from him. She glanced over her shoulder, then nodded. "Yes. He's fine. Um. Okay. Sure."

Holding the phone out to him, she tried to smile. "It's your mother. Someone called her to let her know we were in town together." Leaning closer, she covered the mic and whispered. "She says she's been calling you all morning and just wants to say hi."

"Yeah, right." With a deep breath, he took the device and prepared for a deluge of questions and advice. After the third suggestion that he should move back to his room, he told her that they needed to get Sebastian something to eat. "Yes. I need to eat too, but I can't if I'm talking to you."

"Oh, *mijo*. You should come to the house so I can feed you right."

"I promise I'll be there Sunday."

"I don't see why you can't just move back home. Your room is waiting for you."

"Mom." He didn't bother with all the reasons why he shouldn't move back into his old bedroom.

"Well, anyway, I'm so happy Lilianna has returned home. I love that God has answered my prayers and sent someone with medical experience you will listen to. This makes your mother very happy. I love you."

"I love you too, Mom." And he did, but she was just too much sometimes.

"Please call. I know you want to be all tough and strong, but we worry about you."

"I know. I'll call. I promise." His mother was one of God's many wonders. At four-eleven, she should have been easy to ignore. But she had a presence that commanded attention. After his father's death seventeen years ago, she'd supported her seven children on her preschool teacher's pay. Whether it was a horde of three-year-olds, a rowdy group of middle-school boys, or the chaos of pre-prom drama with teenage girls, she controlled the situation like a four-star general directed their troops in a war zone.

There was no ignoring his mother or oldest sister. Marguerite had inherited their mother's demeanor. Josefina was only eleven months older than him, but that made little difference. He loved them, but they tended to bulldoze anyone in their way when it came to taking care of the people they cared about. They considered Lilianna one of theirs too.

He placed Lilianna's phone on the middle console and started the truck. "Sorry about them."

"Don't worry. Your mother is a force to be reckoned with. She's my inspiration for motherhood."

He chuckled. "Yes. I always know she's got my back. I heard she was a tyrant when I went into surgery. But space can be a beautiful thing too. She has issues with letting go and trusting me. I'm over thirty years old, and she makes me feel as if I'm fifteen and can't be expected to make the right choice."

Laughing, she shook her head. "You've always been the most mature person I knew. You were like twelve going on sixty."

She reached across the console and lightly touched his arm. "Remember the time we had a bonfire on the beach and Eduardo pulled out a box of illegal bottle rockets? You were so mad at him. But, as usual, he wouldn't listen to you. He actually burned himself, and when—" She pinched her lips tight and glanced to the back seat.

Sebastian had his head close to Mack's. They were deep in conversation. She tilted her head back and closed her eyes. "Some stories are best left untold for now." Lifting her head, she looked at her phone. "We have two more hours before we can go to the house. I was so eager to get out of San Antonio that I didn't time our arrival very well. It's such a Eduardo thing to do."

"How about we go to the beach with the new toys? That should kill enough time."

"We're going back to the beach. Yay!" Sebastian lifted his fist in the air.

Her face lit up with a real smile. "The beach it is."

It didn't take them long to return to Pier 9. Lilianna was out of the truck before he shut off the engine. She was helping Sebastian gather some of his new beach toys.

"Are we going to build a sandcastle?" His voice pitched in excitement.

"Bridges was always the best at that." With a quick smile, she took her son's hand in hers and they headed to the beach. She looked over her shoulder. "Can you grab the snacks and drinks?"

He'd do whatever she asked. His mother saw Lilianna's return to Port Del Mar as a blessing. She had no way of knowing that Lilianna Perez had been much more than a family friend to Bridges. He had fallen for her in high school, but his best friend had made the first move.

After basic training, Eduardo had married the only girl Bridges had ever loved. He had successfully buried those feelings so deep they were all but forgotten.

A little over three years ago, they had lost Eduardo in a helicopter accident while he was serving overseas. The honor and respect demanded from Bridges ensured that those unwelcome feelings stay buried. The thought of benefiting in any way from his friend's death made him sick to his stomach.

A week or two with them in town was doable, but two months? Having her this close for that long was going to be more painful than the wound the bullet had left behind.

* * *

Sebastian hadn't wanted to leave the beach, but with the promise of Whataburger, he'd eagerly scrambled to the truck. Lilianna hadn't been so excited to get back in the cab. Each time would make it easier, but the pickup still held too many bittersweet memories of what could never be.

Now her meal stayed in the orange-striped bag on her lap, untouched. She turned and made sure Sebastian wasn't making a mess. "Eduardo never allowed food or drinks in the truck."

Bridges laughed. "I used to tease him all the time about his precious *toro* and pretended to spill all sorts of stuff."

"He was reckless about so many things, but not his baby. He was meticulous when it came to this thing." She had given him such a hard time about his protectiveness over a hunk of metal.

Bridges reached out and grasped her hand. "And you. You and Sebastian were his world. Everything he did was to make a good life for y'all. This truck was never more important than you."

She gave several hard blinks, then smiled at the little boy in the back seat as he shared a fry with Mack. "I know. There are times I feel like I let him down somehow."

His whole face wrinkled in a severe frown. "What? That doesn't make any sense."

"Mom, are we there yet?" Sebastian saved her from making a bigger mess of this whole trip. Bridges didn't want to hear about her self-doubt and insecurities.

"Almost." Views of the bay would pop up on their left side, then there were glimpses of the Gulf between huge grassy dunes on their right. "It's beautiful, though. The ocean is so calming. Are you enjoying staying on the ranch?"

"It's taken me back to one of the best parts of my childhood. All the hours I spent with Dad riding across pastures. I don't miss the cold mornings or the blistering hot afternoons. But I do miss the land and the animals. Damian has a few horses he said I could ride. Maybe we can take Sebastian on a jaunt to the beach. There's a possibility of seeing sea turtles if we ask. The family is working with a foundation that protects critical marine habitats, so the beach is off-limits to the public. We could have it all to ourselves."

The bay faded and vast strips of land surrounded them. Then a row of colorful beach houses in pink, yellow and all shades of blue appeared. Grass-covered dunes were the only thing between the homes and beach. All of them sat high on piers and beams overlooking the Gulf.

"Is that Tito's house?" Sebastian pointed to a large turquoise home with double wraparound decks.

"Oh no. We don't have anything that fancy."

"But I want to stay in that house on the beach," he practically yelled at her.

"Sebastian." She gave him the mom stare, the one she'd learned from Momma Espinoza.

Her son tucked his head, frowning. This attitude was so new.

Turning onto a dirt road, they drove past a row of smaller beach houses and cottages. They were adorably rustic, and one had a welcoming set of rocking chairs.

It also had a fresh coat of yellow paint trimmed in white. Growing up, she had seen it range from blue to pink. The tightness in her throat surprised her. A hazy memory came into sharp focus.

As an eight-year-old, she had clung to the post on the front porch as her mother screamed and slammed doors. Pulling a large animal-print bag behind her, her beautiful mother had stomped down the stairs to a waiting car. Her father had sobbed and begged her to stay.

She closed her eyes against the image. It was so far in the past. She had been close to Sebastian's age.

"Lilianna?" Bridges' voice pulled her back to the present. "Are you okay?"

She nodded and plastered a smile on her face. "Sure. It's just been a while." She got out and went to help Sebastian. "I think I spent more time at the Espinoza's' casa than mine. It's where I met your dad. He lived a few houses down and was there all the time too."

"Yep. My mom's house is at the end of this road. It was the go-to place for hanging out because she's a strong believer in feeding everyone."

Sebastian tossed a fry into his mouth. "I know your mom. She's Angie's grandma." He wrinkled his nose. "Does she live here too?"

He didn't look happy about it.

"Whenever they visited San Antonio, you got along with Marguerite's kids. She lives next door to my mom. I thought you liked playing with them."

"Josh is okay." He shrugged, then ran to Bridges and took his hand. "So that's where you live?"

"I don't live with my mom anymore."

"Why not? I want to always live with mine. You could live with us."

He laughed. "Thanks, but I have my own house. I'm not far. Just a few miles down the main road is the Diamondback Ranch. It's close. You can come out to see me, and I can stop by anytime I go into town."

She stepped into the cozy cottage. Her mom had wanted more, but her father had lived his dream as a fishing boat captain. The interior looked a little worn, and the decor was a cheesy seaside theme for the tourists who rented the house, but it was neat and clean. The fishing nets and plastic pelicans would come down soon. She liked the soft colors of blue and coral, though.

Sebastian didn't move past the door.

"You have the room with the bunk beds."

With a disinterested nod, he went to investigate.

Bridges passed her and put the groceries on the tall, square table that was pushed against the wall. "Wow. Strange how I don't remember it being this small."

"You were three feet shorter the last time you were here."

He chuckled. "True." Hands on his hips, he scanned the area, then went to the sink and opened the cabinet. "Needs a little touch-up, but it looks to be in good shape."

"Knock, knock." The door opened, and Bridges's oldest sister poked her head around the screen door. Thick braids of dark hair rested on her shoulders. Her smile was warm, and she carried a large casserole dish. "Hello! Is it okay if we come in?" She avoided her brother's glare. "We saw y'all pull up and wanted to welcome you back to Port Del Mar with a proper greeting."

"I've lived in my house in San Antonio for six years and I don't think any of my neighbors have stopped by. This is so nice." Why was the kind gesture getting her all emotional? She should have come home years ago.

Marguerite gave her a sheepish smile. "I have a King

Ranch chicken casserole." She lifted in the air. "And a variety of *pan dulce* fresh from my *panaderia*."

Bridges's sister owned a Mexican bakery in town, and the aroma from her sweet breads was making Lilianna's mouth water.

Lilianna took the casserole and turned away to the kitchen island to collect herself. "Thank you so much. One of the things I'm most looking forward to is finally getting to visit your bakery."

"Hi!" Marguerite's two younger children, a boy and girl close to Sebastian's age, appeared at her side. Her oldest daughter, Angie, was hovering in the background with the box from the bakery.

"Angie, Nica and Josh wanted to say hi to Sebastian and insisted we bring him the treats."

Bridges took the box and went the few short steps to the kitchen. The look he gave his older sister had Lilianna biting her lip not to laugh. It was a surprise that his mother wasn't here too.

"Let me get him." Going to the bedroom, Lilianna found Sebastian on the top bunk. "Hey. We have some guests who want to say hi to you. Angie, Nica and Josh are here."

He kept his head down. "No."

Her heart broke. What had happened to her sweet little guy? She didn't want to force him to visit, but she couldn't allow him to sulk in the room alone. That wasn't healthy either. Going to the bed, she touched his leg. "Are you sad? What's wrong? You can tell me anything, baby."

"Nothing."

Bridges braced his arm on the door frame. "Everything okay?"

"I don't want to talk to people."

Walking to stand next to her, Bridges held his hand palm up and wiggled his fingers. "Come on out. You can stay right with me. Okay?"

With a nod, Sebastian stood and, without warning, jumped at Bridges from the upper bunk. With an *oof*, Bridges staggered but kept his balance.

"Sebastian!" Lilianna grabbed for him to relieve Bridges.

Her son's eyes went wide. "Oh no. Did I hurt you? I'm sorry."

"I'm fine." His voice was hoarse.

Sebastian slid to the floor to stand between them. "I forgot. I didn't mean to hurt you."

"I'm okay. We've established that it takes a lot more than that to damage me. You have friends here. Not yet in town for a full day and already people are knocking on your door. You're one popular guy."

Sebastian giggled but kept his hand tightly grasped in Lilianna's.

Josh rushed into the room. "Hey, you've got the coolest swing and fort in your backyard. I've always wanted to play on it, but Momma said we couldn't. Can we go see it?"

Sebastian squeezed closer to her. Bridges kneeled in front of them. "I'll go with you. I didn't know you had your own playground. How cool is that? Want to?"

Her son's big sad eyes, full of doubt, tore at her heart. "I'll be right here if you need me. I'm not leaving," she said.

With a nod from Sebastian and a wide grin from Bridges, they moved to the kitchen door. Under the rental manager's advice, they had added an outdoor entertainment area with a firepit and patio to make it more attractive to vacationers. It also included a large, multilevel play structure with a fort, swings, slides and climbing walls.

"Bridges." She yelled his name. "Remember your injury. No catching flying children or swinging them." She narrowed her gaze at him.

"Yes, ma'am."

Marguerite gave him the same "mom look" as she leaned against the counter and crossed her arms. "If I'd said that, he would have done it just to prove he didn't have to listen to me. Little brothers are such pains. They act as if ensuring someone is healthy and safe is fussing."

"He's not so little anymore."

He winked at her as he held the door open for the kids. His lopsided grin just about stole her heart. No, this was Bridges. There couldn't be any heart-stealing. She was just tired. New subject.

She gave Marguerite her full attention. "We need to get all caught up. The most shocking news I heard was that Damian is married now." Damian De La Rosa had been friends with her husband and Bridges. They were all military men. A war injury had left him a double amputee, and he had become a shut-in on the ranch.

Marguerite chuckled. "Yep. Could have knocked the whole town over with that unexpected turn of events. It's his old cabin that Bridges is living in now. Lately, Port Del Mar seems to be a good place for new beginnings and finding it with that right person." The shorter woman grinned and nudged Lilianna.

"Oh no." She shot a horrified look out the window, where she could see Bridges playing with the kids. "It's not like that. We're not like that at all. He's Eduardo's best friend." She made herself busy, arranging the groceries she and Bridges had brought from town.

"Sorry. Y'all just kind of give off a couple vibe. I really didn't mean to freak you out." A soft touch brought her attention back to Marguerite. The woman was standing next to her. "My mom might have said something about..."

Lilianna gasped. His mother. What if she had the crazy idea of playing matchmaker? She wouldn't do that to her, would she? Who was she kidding? That was exactly what Momma Espinoza would do. How humiliating.

"I'm truly sorry. I didn't mean to upset you."

"I'm probably being oversensitive. But then again, your mother does tend to think she can fix everything for her kids if they would just listen."

"A condition almost all mothers struggle with. Mom is so happy that you're here. I mean, who better than an emergency room nurse to look after *mijo*?" She put the casserole in the refrigerator.

Lilianna was starting to sweat. "Oh, look. There's coffee. I need coffee. Want some?" She dropped a pod in the maker.

"No. I'm good. The church has been praying for you and Sebastian. We thought you'd come home sooner. You know Mom thinks of you as one of her daughters."

The coffee wasn't moving fast enough. "Your mom has been the closest thing I have to a mother. She's amazing. She has seven kids by birth and still took on more."

"In these parts, parents still fight over her. Everyone wants their child in her preschool class. I love her, but I admit she does have a problem with knowing when to stop plotting. Or, as she calls it, *mothering*."

Lilianna didn't bother pointing out that Marguerite had the same problem.

Her phone dinged with a notification. "Oh, it's the car. It's going to be ready in another hour."

"That's good news. I know you've had a long day. I'll get the kids and head out. Unless you need anything else?"

"No. I'm good. Thank you." They headed to the backyard.

Her heart lightened. This had turned into a good day. *Thank you, God, for taking care of us and knowing our needs better than we did.*

"What a pretty backyard."

"I'd love to add hydrangeas. Like the beautiful ones your mom has. They've always made me think of home."

"Maybe we could go get some at the nursery."

"No. I won't be here long enough."

"Let me know if you change your mind." She clapped to get her kids' attention. "Time to go home. We have animals to feed before I start dinner. *Vamonos*."

"Mom! Josh says I can go with him and help."

"I'm glad you want to, but you'll need to come with me. When we get back—"

"No! I don't."

"Sebastian," she said through clenched teeth, then forced herself to relax. Why was he doing this now?

Bridges went to the wall where Sebastian was climbing and lifted him off. "Hey. You're not arguing with your mom, are you?"

With a grunt, he sat her son down and rubbed at his chest. At this rate he was never going to fully heal.

"Bridges. You hurt yourself again."

His cell rang. He frowned. "Hello?" Phone to his ear, he stepped away from them. "Hey, Andres. Or I guess I should say *Officer Sanchez*. What can I do for you?"

Lilianna's gut clenched. Why would the local police be calling him? He had moved far enough away that she couldn't hear, but his expression indicated bad news.

"What do you think it's about?" Her heart slammed against her chest.

Marguerite moved away from the play structure with a worried glance at her brother. "Not sure."

Bridges lowered the phone from his ear but just stood staring at it. He was still over by the fence. With a glance to see that the kids were happily occupied, she went to him.

Her blood rushed through her body, leaving her oddly light and empty. "Bridges?"

He looked at her, then shook his head. "I don't understand." He rubbed the back of his neck as he spoke into the phone again. "He says I'm his father...? Now? You need me to come pick him up now?"

Father? One part of her wanted to collapse in relief. Everyone was fine. But the other half wanted to yell "What is going on?"

"Is everything okay?" Marguerite came up next to her.

Bridges shot her a look that made it clear he didn't want his sister to know what was happening.

"Oh. Um. Yes." That was smooth. She wasn't any good at lying, and he knew that. "More bad news on my car. He's clearing it up."

"Go ahead and let Sebastian come with us, and y'all

go into town to find out what's up. Kids aren't good at waiting."

"Thank you." Bridges had a son that was with the police? How did she not know? Apparently, his mother and sister didn't either.

She watched him. Judging by his reaction, he hadn't known either. He looked at her, and his eyes had an edge of panic to them she had never seen before.

"You know what? That sounds like a good idea. Thank you. Let's go tell the kids."

Going to his side, she put a reassuring hand on his arm. Whatever it was, he had to know she was here for him.

Chapter Four

Bridges blinked. He couldn't have heard right. "My son?"

"We found an unattended minor asleep under the pier." Officer Andres Sanchez repeated the fact again in a slow, calm matter that didn't fit the situation. "The kid looks dehydrated and hungry, but he won't say anything other than he wants his father. Claims he's yours."

He lowered his voice, speaking in a friendly tone, not as an officer of the law. "Espinoza, he has all the appearances of a runaway. We're on the way to the station. We told him we'd call, and that you'd meet us there. That's the only reason he willingly got in the car." He lowered his voice. "Do you have a son your family doesn't know about?"

"I'm headed there now. Can I speak with him?" His brain raced in circles. There was no way. Who was his mother?"

"Hello?" He sounded older than Bridges had expected. "Is this Bridges Espinoza?"

"Can you tell me your name?"

"Not till I see you. I don't know who you are." There

was a strong underpinning of rage. "Are you coming to get me?"

"Yes. I'm about fifteen minutes out of town. Get some food and water, and we'll talk when I get there."

"I'm waiting for you." The phone went dead. His mind wasn't working. He just stared at the device in his hand.

"Bridges? Bridges."

He looked up and met the eyes of the woman he'd known most of his life. He just stared at her.

"Bridges. Are you okay?"

"That was Sanchez." He lowered his voice, making sure his sister wouldn't hear. "They found a kid under the pier. A twelve-year-old boy. The only thing he told Sanchez was that I was his father." He knew there was no way the kid could be his, but why was he telling that to the police? Where was his mother? Better yet, who was his mother?

She took the phone. "I heard. So, you didn't know about him?" Her words were slow, and he still had a hard time processing.

He shook his head. His gaze scanned the area, looking for an answer as to what was happening.

A gentle touch grounded him. He needed facts.

Her fingers squeezed his arm. "We'll go to town together. We can visit with the boy, then get my car. Sebastian is staying with Marguerite." She walked away from him. He wanted to stop her and hold her until this sick feeling went away. Instead, he left the safe backyard.

He stood next to the big truck and leaned his head against the glass. The coolness helped calm the chaos in his brain. If he was going to make any sense of this, he needed to pull it together.

"Do you want me to drive?" Lilianna stood next to him, her soft hand on his arm.

Shaking his head, he opened the door and got in. He'd told the kid he'd be there in fifteen.

The loud clashing sound in his head contrasted with the silence in the cab. He was going to explode if he didn't release some of the pressure.

"Maybe he's not yours. Could it be a scam?"

He knew the kid wasn't his, but did the kid really think he was his father or was it some sort of con? Either someone was using the boy, or they had lied to him. "I need to talk to him, hear what he says. You'll go with me, right? Working in the ER, you've developed a quick read of people. Between the two of us, we'll figure it out."

"Of course. How old is he?"

"Twelve."

"You were in Georgia. Who did you date in your early Army life?"

No one. "But the kid's here in Texas." His fingers gripped the steering wheel. "Where's his mother? Why was he alone on the beach, sleeping under the pier?" He took a deep breath. "Once we see him, talk to him, I'll have a better idea of what's going on."

He needed a plan of action. Meet the boy. Get his name and information. His mother's name.

In less than ten minutes, he'd pull up to the Port Del Mar Police station and come face-to-face with a child claiming to be his son.

The last time Lilianna had walked into the Port Del Mar police station, it had been back in high school to pick up Eduardo for scrambling letters on the local business marquees. It was startling to see so many of the same faces. Lori Eagleton greeted them at the front desk. She hugged Lilianna, her head barely reaching Lilianna's shoulder. "Oh, sweet girl, it's been too long." She stepped back, but her fingers stayed gripped around Lilianna's wrist. "Sorry to hear about your daddy. He was such a hardworking man. And of course, poor Eduardo. You and that sweet little boy of yours have been in our prayers. Coming home is the best thing you can do."

"Thank you." Her throat burned at the outpouring of love from a woman she hadn't even thought about in years.

Bridges put his arm around her and gave the older woman his best smile. "We'll be at church Sunday. So, we're here to meet with Officer Sanchez."

"Oh, yes. Yes. He said to let you know he'd be in the conference room. That poor boy, out on the street all by himself. I made sure he took a shower." She wrinkled her nose. "He had one change of clothes. They weren't much better than the ones he was wearing. So, I gave him one of our T-shirts." She shook her head. "I hope you can help him. Do you know what's going on?"

Sanchez was keeping quiet on the reason the boy was here.

Stepping out of her reach, Lilianna smiled at her and took Bridges's hand. "Thank you so much for the prayers and help." Lori was a dear, sweet woman and always the first to reach out and help whenever needed, but she could also talk the ears off fresh corn. And she prided herself in being a great source of information. She claimed it wasn't gossip if it was true. Lilianna didn't want to give her more to talk about than she already had.

With a polite nod to Mrs. Eagleton, Bridges took Lilianna's hand, led her around the desk. His fingers gripped hers as they silently headed down the carpeted hallway. He paused at the door before opening it, then he stepped to the side so she could enter first.

At a long oval table, a boy sat with his arms crossed. Despite the Texas heat, he was wearing a dark hoodie. Trying to blend into his surroundings. Goal to be invisible. His black hair was pushed back, still wet. Dark curls were falling forward as it started to dry. Anger radiated from him, his dark eyes daring anyone to touch him.

She had seen that look too many times on runaways and homeless minors they treated in the ER. The hostility was just barbed wire wrapped around a scared kid. The instinct to give him a hug and offer comfort was strong, but she stood to the side.

In front of the boy was a water bottle, a vending machine sandwich, chips and a candy bar. All untouched. Andres nodded at them and stepped forward to shake Bridges's hand. She hadn't seen him since high school. He was taller and looked as if he had seen too much of the world. He had talked of making the Air Force his career.

The boy sat up when he saw Bridges. "You're my father." The intensity of the stark vulnerability and hope pulled at her heart. Whatever the truth was, this boy believed he was Bridges's son.

Approaching the boy, Bridges sat in the chair next to him. He glanced at her, then at the seat on the other side of him.

"Who's she? Your wife?" He glared at her as if she was about to take his last thread of hope.

"I'm Bridges Espinoza. This is Lilianna. A family friend. What's your name?"

With a shaking hand, he pulled a picture out of his hoodie pocket and laid it on the table in front of Bridges. "I'm Cooper Jennings. That's my mom, Kathy. You remember her, right?" He swallowed visibly. The boy's brown eyes pleaded for him to remember. Then his gaze darted to Andres who was opening the door to leave.

"Don't call them." He stood, as if he could do anything to stop Andres from making the call. He looked more frightened than angry.

"Don't call who?" Bridges asked.

The boy sat down and closed up, his mouth in a tight line.

"I'm not calling anybody. I'm just going to check to see who might be looking for you. Before I make contact, I'll come back and talk to y'all. I suggest you take this opportunity to tell Bridges everything you can—and stick to the truth. Anything else will just complicate your life." He left them alone.

Bridges picked up the picture. A beautiful red-haired woman, with one arm looped around Bridges and the other around Eduardo, stood with her head tilted, blowing a kiss to the camera. He flipped it over. In neat print was his name and a date. It matched with his time in Georgia.

Lilianna moved her gaze to Bridges. She studied his face as he considered the photo again. She couldn't read him at all. Did he remember the boy's mother? Was Cooper his son?

There was a part of her that wanted it to be true, for the sake of this lost child. Bridges would make a terrific father, and his whole family would sweep in and love this boy the way they had done for her and Eduardo.

In the silence, the boy fidgeted. "My mother told me all about you. Y'all dated when you were training for the Army in Georgia. She said you were the best guy, and that if you knew about me, you'd…" He tucked his head.

"I'd what?" Putting the picture down, Bridges lowered his head, trying to make eye contact.

Cooper shrugged.

"Why don't you eat and tell me where your mother is now? I'd like to talk to her. Did you come all the way from Georgia?"

"I walked from Houston."

Lilianna bit back a gasp. That had to be close to eight miles. He had been in so much danger.

As if it were no big deal, Cooper went for the candy bar first. He talked around a bite of chocolate, nuts and caramel. "She said you met in Georgia, but you left before she knew about me. She came to Texas to find you. On the road, she met Danny. He was a trucker that lived in Houston and they got married. That's where I was born. My birth certificate says my father is Daniel Garza. I thought he was my father for a long time until I was seven. Him and my mom broke up, and she told me about you."

"Where's your mom now?"

Lilianna realized he had not acknowledged that he remembered the woman or that Cooper could be his.

Making himself even smaller, Cooper balled up in the chair with his chin to his chest. He closed his eyes. But she had seen the sheen. He was about to cry. Moving around Bridges, Lilianna went to the other side of Cooper and laid a hand on his arm. This boy needed love.

She had a horrible feeling about his answer. "Cooper. We're here and we want to help. Can you tell us where your mother is?"

"She's dead." His voice broke. "They say she killed herself, but she didn't. It was an accident. She wouldn't have left me. Not on purpose."

Lilianna wanted to pull him into her arms and fit him tightly against her heart. He tugged away and sat up straighter. "The last time she called me, she said she had found my father, and as soon as she talked to him, we'd all be together. She was happy and clean. She promised me she was clean.

"She told me you were from Port Del Mar. She was going to visit you and tell you about me." He turned away. "She was right. When they gave me a box of her things, I found the picture. I knew if I could get here, I'd find you." The kid gave them the saddest smile she had ever seen. "It worked."

"Who were you staying with?" Bridges's voice was low and smooth. "There has to be someone we need to call."

Cooper's lips curled in distaste. "No one is missing me. I'm on my own."

The doorknob clicked, and they all turned. Officer Andres Sanchez sat down across from them. "What has Cooper told you?"

Bridges gave the boy a long look, then sat back in his chair. "His mother is Kathy Jennings. She told him I was his father. She's passed away."

"Could he be yours?"

"I was in Georgia at the correct time, and he has a picture of us together. What did you find out?"

Lilianna narrowed her eyes at Bridges, trying to fig-

ure out what he was doing. He had been very careful
not to deny or acknowledge his connection to Kathy
and Cooper.

Turning from him, she looked to Andres. "What did
you discover?"

"He's in state custody. He's been in and out for the
last four years."

"My mom was a good mom. She just had some really bad boyfriends, but she didn't lie to me. She tried
real hard to be a good mom." His nostrils flared and his
hands clenched into fists.

Andres leaned forward. "I'm sure she did. Sometimes life hands out problems that are bigger than we can
handle alone." His gaze went to Lilianna, then Bridges.
"How long ago did you run away?"

As the fight left him, the boy's shoulders slumped.
"After the last day of school, I headed this way. I like
walking."

Fear for what could have happened to him twisted
her heart.

Andres nodded and sat back. With a pointed glare at
Bridges, he said, "No one has reported him missing."

Understanding horrified her. The people who should
be caring for him hadn't informed anyone that he was
gone. The world could be a very dangerous place for a
twelve-year-old boy alone.

She was about to offer her home as shelter, but before
saying anything, she looked at Bridges. They were here
because the boy claimed to be his. There was no way he
would abandon Cooper. His mouth was in a hard line
as he studied his hands. She knew he was analyzing all
the information and options. That was how he worked.
But his face was unreadable, and if he didn't say some-

thing soon, the boy would bolt. He looked like a rabbit that didn't know if he was going to be fed or eaten.

Bridges held the boy's gaze. "Did they hurt you, your foster parents?"

"No. They just didn't care what I did as long as I didn't bother them or get in trouble."

With a guttural sound from deep in his throat, Bridges shook his head. "Did they know you were coming to find me?"

"I told them I wanted to come to Port Del Mar to look for you. They said they didn't have the time for a vacation, and that it would be a waste of money. Todd, the man, said if you didn't want me when I was little and cute, why would you suddenly want me when I was..." He jerked his face to the wall. His jaw was going back and forth.

Silence hung in the room for what seemed like hours.

Bridges stood and went to the window.

Lilianna glanced between the men. "No one has reported him missing from foster care. That means someone is still getting checks. That's not the kind of family that he should be going back to." She knew lots of foster parents. Most went above and beyond for the children in their care, but occasionally, she came across this type of situation and it burned her gut. These kids were already the most vulnerable children. They needed stability and extra care.

Arms crossed, Bridges faced them. He was leaning on the windowsill. "So, what can we do now? He's not going back to that family."

"I'll report to Child Protection Services and let them know what we have." Sanchez twisted his mouth to the side. "If Bridges is his father—"

"He is!" Cooper stood and slammed his fist into the table. "My mom's not a liar."

Ignoring the outburst, Sanchez continued, "I would turn him over to you. It would also be the easiest fix for CPS. They prefer to keep families together if possible."

"I can stay with Bridges." He went to the window but kept his distance. "I don't want to go back. Please let me stay with you."

There was hope in the dark eyes that had too much of the world in them for his young age.

"I'm foster trained and certified. We had some incidents at the hospital with newborns being left in emergency situations, so I took them until we could get them situated into a safe place. If CPS needs more time to work out the documentation that Bridges is his father, I can keep him until we get that figured out."

"I have a letter from my mom giving me all the details. It explains why he didn't know." Cooper picked up the threadbare backpack. It had checkered duct tape holding the only strap together. Pulling out a plastic bag, he gently laid it on the table, as if it were a precious gem. "Will this help?"

The yearning in the boy's voice made it clear he thought this was his only option.

Sanchez sighed and took the evidence the boy offered. He looked at Bridges. "It will, if you agree. Do you affirm that Cooper is your son?"

Bridges looked at the boy. "I want custody of him. We'll make sure that he's safe and taken care of."

"If you give me a copy of your ID, I'll contact CPS. Might as well give me yours too, in order to ensure this goes off without any problems." He held his hand out to Lilianna.

As she pulled her credentials from her bag, she glanced at Cooper. He didn't seem as scared, but he still looked as if he wasn't sure what was happening.

The boy needed so much, but they could start by furnishing him with some basics. "Would we be able to take him to eat?"

Bridges nodded. "We'll bring him back here when we're done. Then, hopefully, you'll have everything settled."

"Sounds like a good idea. I'll call if I need anything."

Bridges walked to the table. "You want some fresh clothes and a hamburger?"

"Can we get the hamburger first?"

With a laugh, Bridges patted the kid on the shoulder. "It'll be a quick trip to the mercantile. Don't you think?" He looked at her for confirmation.

"It won't take long. I have a son that hates shopping. I'm not much into it myself. But you must admit that clean shorts and a good pair of shoes would be nice."

"Okay," he mumbled.

When was the last time he'd gone shopping for new clothes? Bridges led the way to his truck. Cooper stayed close to him.

She followed. There was something very familiar about the boy. But she couldn't imagine Bridges leaving a child behind.

The plan to come home and reconnect with her son was going well, but she hadn't expected to reconnect with Bridges. And Bridges's son? Life was full of surprises.

What other surprises did the summer hold?

Chapter Five

For the second time that day, Bridges opened the door to leave the old-fashioned mercantile. "The Painted Dolphin is my favorite place to eat. It's just a short walk across the street and down the block."

Cooper nodded and gripped his backpack, which was slung over his left shoulder. He had been wide-eyed at the variety of items in the general store. As promised, Lilianna had had them in and out in under fifteen minutes.

"I asked people at the pier about you. No one knew you."

"That's because I don't live here anymore." He stopped at the truck. "And people that do know me would be cautious about giving private info. Put your backpack in the truck, and I'll lock it."

Panic flashed in Cooper's eyes, and he pulled the worn-out canvas bag closer to him. "I'd rather keep it."

Bridges acted as if it were no big deal and moved toward the restaurant. "It's been too long since I've eaten their mac and cheese. It's my favorite."

Cooper stopped. "Wait. You don't live here? But my mom said…"

"I'm from here, but after I got out of the Army, I took a job in Oklahoma."

Lilianna gave Cooper her sweetest smile. Bridges looked away. He had to. That smile made him want things he couldn't have. And right now, everything was even messier than normal.

"You are so fortunate that he's here. He was shot, so he's home recovering."

"You were shot?" The kid scanned his body like he couldn't believe it. "But you just said you were out of the Army. Where'd you get shot?"

"I'm a police officer now. I was shot in the left shoulder. It's not that bad, but I had to have surgery." His mother always said that God had a reason for everything. He wouldn't be here to help this kid if the shooting hadn't happened. His mom would have been called. She wouldn't have hesitated to take him home. A groan escaped his chest. An angry preteen was the last thing his mother needed at this point in her life.

He couldn't turn his back on an abandoned kid. It went against everything his parents taught him. Keeping him close would give Bridges a chance to find the truth of why the kid thought he was his father.

"How were you shot? In a drug bust?" The boy's voice was too excited.

"No. I was helping a woman leave her home when her husband showed up and shot at us."

"Did he shoot his wife?"

"Nope, just me." The man had been taken down by his partner, but he didn't think the boy needed the details.

Cooper kicked a pebble on the sidewalk. "What if they don't let me stay with you? I don't want to go back to the Barnharts'." He jabbed his fist into the front pocket of his new hoodie. His jaw was tight. "I'll run away again. They can't force me to stay."

The kid's whole body was tense as he fought the tears.

"Acting tough will only get you so far, and the streets are a nasty place to live. Between me and Lilianna, we got you covered, okay? If you get scared, just talk to us, don't run. Promise?"

The boy's nod was coupled with a shrug. Cooper had had too many disappointments to believe any good would come from this.

The bigger problem was the kid's real father. Who was he, and what was the best way to go about finding him?

At the restaurant, they were seated outside next to the water. Boats sailed by. At the end of the pier, a pirate ship was anchored. Elijah De La Rosa, his friend's cousin and owner of the ship and restaurant, came to their table.

He greeted them, then smiled at Cooper. "Glad to see you're safe."

Cooper got quiet. "He's the guy that gave me food from the kitchen." He narrowed his eyes. "You said you didn't know Bridges Espinoza."

"You wouldn't tell me your name, so I said I couldn't give you any information."

"You called the police."

The accusation was sharp, but Elijah just gave him an easy grin. "I did, and now you're eating with the person you were looking for. It seemed to work out well."

Bridges grinned. "Mr. De La Rosa is the owner. He owns that pirate ship too." He gestured to it.

Elijah gave them a rueful grin. "I'm glad you found him."

"You own the pirate ship? Really?" The hostility faded, leaving a curious twelve-year-old in its place. "That's so cool. Can I get a closer look while we're waiting for the food?"

Bridges looked at Lilianna for guidance. She knew more about this kind of thing than he did.

"I can walk him over," Elijah offered. "The crew is cleaning after a birthday party. If you don't mind? I do kind of owe him, since I called the cops."

Bridges nodded, a little uneasy about letting the boy out of his sight.

Lilianna patted his hand. "We can see him from here, and I think he's getting restless with all the sitting he's done today." With the first real smile Bridges had seen, Cooper followed Elijah to the ship.

Not taking his eyes off the boy claiming to be his son, he nodded. "This is good timing. We need to talk."

She narrowed her eyes as if she could look past his skin and into his heart. "What's been going on in your head? You've been very careful with your words. He's not yours, is he?"

"No." He was relieved that she knew him well enough to know that he wouldn't father a child without knowing. "But I don't want him to be lost in the system. That kid truly believes I'm his father. I went out and did a little dating, but I was never in a relationship."

"But there's the picture with your name. Do you remember her?"

"Not at all."

"There's no way to know who his father could be?"

"I don't have a clue. But after meeting him, I couldn't say that to him. Can you imagine what he'd do if the man he believes to be his father turned his back on him? This should give us time to figure something out. I couldn't hand him back over to people that don't care about him."

He pulled out the picture Cooper had given him. "Looks like a local hangout the guys went to on the weekends. I only was there once or twice."

"You have too much of your mother in you to walk away from anyone in trouble." She sighed and looked at the photo. She touched Eduardo's face. "He might have known. He could tell you someone's life story after one meeting. People told him everything, and he listened."

She pulled her hands back and turned to the ship. "Maybe she didn't know who his father was. You're a nice guy she liked, and she thought you'd make a good dad." She shrugged. "There's no way to know why she said it. She didn't try too hard to find you."

"Not at first. But this last year, it looks as if it was her mission."

"After all the years of saying your name, she could have started to believe the lie she created. If drugs were involved, there's no telling her state of mind."

"Once we get the custody cleared up, we'll figure out the best way to move forward."

"What if they require a DNA test?"

Bridges leaned back and blew out a long puff of air. "That's the million-dollar question. We'll deal with it then."

A soft breeze came off the Gulf and played with her hair. His chest tightened at the thought of pushing it back. Having her this close was not good for either of them. She just didn't know it. He cleared his throat. "Thank you for coming with me. After we eat, I'll take you to your car. You don't need to wait around with us."

"Oh no. You're not getting rid of me that fast. We're in this together."

Together. That was why he needed to step back from her. *Together* was never going to happen the way he imagined, and she'd be shocked that he ever thought of her romantically. In her world, they were friends and would never be more. Out of respect for Eduardo, it couldn't go further.

"Listen, Lilianna, you need to get Sebastian and settle in. I've got this. You don't need to get wrapped up in my messy life."

With her chin down, she glared at him. "You listen to me. I'm not abandoning that boy any more than you are, and you, my friend, need my help whether you are willing to admit it or not. I know your normal plan of action is to tackle any problem alone. You can't do that this time."

She had no idea how much truth she spoke. He needed her too much, and that wasn't good for either of them. If he was to be a man of honor and integrity, like his father had raised him to be, he'd make sure she was safe and far from him.

He looked away from her stormy eyes and out over the calm sea. His father had taught him that a man took care of the people he loved. He didn't risk their happiness to lessen his own burdens.

A friendly waitress put their order on the table. Lilianna smiled as she looked over his shoulder. "You have perfect timing. The food has arrived."

Cooper's dark skin was flushed, and he started coughing as he slid onto the bench next to her. She placed the back of her hand on his forehead. "Cooper, how do you feel? You might have a fever." She moved the cup of water closer to him. "You're probably dehydrated."

"I'm fine." He stuffed fries into his mouth with one hand and slipped several others into his pocket with the other.

Bridges was about to tell him that he didn't have to hoard food, but Lilianna shook her head.

"I'm fine." Cooper repeated, but he didn't move away from her touch. There was a yearning in his eyes that he couldn't hide. The pain in the boy was so palpable that Bridges's chest hurt.

He knew how it felt to believe you were isolated with no one to turn to for help.

"You need more water." He slid the glass toward the boy.

Bridges's phone went off. "It's Sanchez."

All the fear was back in Cooper's eyes. Lilianna put an arm around him and said something Bridges couldn't hear.

"Espinoza here."

"So, everything is good to go. Congratulations, you're a father. There's no reason to come in. Lori has cleared all the details with the CPS worker. She'll email you. I gave them both your and Lilianna's information. They'll do a follow-up. They're so slammed I'm sure it's a relief to have an easy solution."

"Thank you."

"I'm glad this all worked out. Sorry that you had to

find out you had a son this way. That has to be tough. Call if you need anything."

"Will do." He disconnected, then just stared at his phone for a bit. That was it. He had temporary custody of a twelve-year-old boy he'd just met.

A month ago, he'd had a simple life. He'd complained about being a little lonely and bored. God had taken care of that.

Now he was back in his hometown, Lilianna was sitting across from him, and he had responsibility for a child. A child who thought he was his father. How had his life gotten so complicated so quickly? His mother's voice in his head reminded him to be careful what you pray for. God might just give it to you.

"Bridges?" Lilianna's voice pulled him out of his brain fog.

Taking a deep breath, he looked at the two sets of eyes staring at him as if he had all the answers. He had stepped into this role, so he needed to man up real fast. "Good news. We're all set. Cooper, you're coming home with me."

The kid pulled back. "You don't seem real happy about it. Can I just go with her?"

Crossing his arms in front of him, Bridges leaned forward. "Sorry. It's all been crazy fast. You've known about me for a while, but this is all new to me. I'm glad you found me, and everything is going to be okay. I promise."

Cooper's lips curled in an unpleasant expression. "Don't make promises you can't keep."

"I don't. You came looking for me, and you found me. I don't know what is going to happen. This might be temporary, but I promise, you are with us until it gets worked out one way or another."

"One way or another? You're my father. Are you trying to pass me off already?"

"No. There are details we don't have yet. But for now, you have the Espinoza clan. We don't walk away from someone that needs us. It includes a very bossy grandmother and several aunts, uncles and cousins. Like my mother says all the time, be careful what you pray for."

The boy's face paled.

Lilianna chuckled. "It's going to be fine. They're good people. You can count on them to always do the right thing."

Cooper looked down. "Um. I need to go to the bathroom."

Bridges glanced to the large arrow that pointed to the restroom. "Okay. But no running away now." He winked, trying to lighten the mood. "It's too late."

"Oh no, I just—"

"It's okay. I'm teasing you. I'll get the rest of our food to go, then we'll take Lilianna to get her car."

As soon as Cooper was out of earshot, Lilianna took his hand. He had to steady his heartbeat and focus on her words instead of her touch. "Have you called your mother? You could go with me when I pick up Sebastian. They need to be introduced."

"Today has been a lot to process for both of us. I think I'll just pick up Mack at your place and head home. I'll call my mother and promise to go over for lunch tomorrow. Taking him tonight seems odd when we haven't even gotten to know each other. The kid might not like me once he does."

"There's nothing to not like. But I do agree about waiting for tomorrow to meet your mother. You need to explain things to her. Of all people, she'll understand what you're doing."

He rubbed the bridge of his nose where a headache was starting to form. "I don't have a clue what I'm doing. What if I'm making it worse? It's easy now, but what happens when he finds out I'm not his father. That man has a right to know he has a son."

"Right now, he needs us. You're doing a great thing. You're helping a kid who's all alone in the world. I knew I couldn't leave him once I heard his story. You've stepped up and made it easier for everyone to give him a safe place. You have such a big heart, Bridges. You're more like your mother than you're willing to admit."

He snorted. "This has nothing to do with my mom. The boy has nowhere else to go. Anyone would have taken him in."

"That's not true and you know it. Most people would walk away, grateful the kid wasn't their problem. Giving him a temporary home is not an easy thing to do, but it's the right thing to do. You, Bridges Espinoza, are a good man."

He wasn't, but arguing with her was pointless. So he smiled and waited for Cooper to return. He was going to have to explain this all to his mother. Man, what had he gotten himself into now?

Tomorrow he'd deal with his family. What he didn't know how to handle was Lilianna being so tangled up in his life.

Feelings he'd thought long buried were resurfacing with each contact. There had to be a way to keep an emotional distance while still helping her like he'd promised Eduardo.

Guilt was a heavy burden, but it was one he would have to carry undercover. He should be used to it by now.

Chapter Six

Big Mack barked a greeting to Sebastian as they entered the backyard the next morning. The boys had met yesterday but still were tentative with each other. The German shepherd mix ran back and forth between Cooper and Sebastian, nudging them and doing what Bridges thought of as a wellness check Mack did whenever he'd been separated from him. Now that little routine included the boys.

He smiled at the thought of Mack seeing them as part of his pack, his family.

Lilianna had her hand on Sebastian's shoulder. "Why don't you take Cooper and show him the tree house?"

"Okay," he mumbled. Mack went with them.

She watched them climb the wall and disappear into the fort that was built into the tree. She smiled at him and pulled at his arm. "Come sit down. Relax. Your mom is going to take to him like she does everyone that comes her way."

Sebastian was inside the fort, waving at them with Cooper at his side. Then he pointed out landmarks to his new friend.

"I have a good feeling about the boys getting along." Settling onto the comfy-looking outdoor furniture, she patted the empty space next to her.

He had a glimpse of a future where they were a family, and his throat closed up. A family with Sebastian and Lilianna was a fantasy that would never happen. Tendrils of the idea burrowed into his heart. It was going to be painful when he had to excavate that little dream. He'd be smart to not allow them to take root. He'd be heading back to Oklahoma soon. Would Cooper be going with him? There was so much uncertainty right now. Why couldn't God just send him a direct message? It would be so much easier.

"Have you told him that you're not his father?"

"No. I'm thinking he would freak and run."

"You're going to have to tell your mother the truth."

"But we don't know the truth. So how do I explain all this?"

"If anyone understands taking in a kid that needs you, it's your mother. Y'all can lay the groundwork for Cooper to hear the news that you're not his father. Talk to her."

He let his head fall back. "How about I don't and say I did? Better yet, you go talk to my mother, and I'll stay here with the boys and hide in the tree house."

"No hiding. Talk to Cooper. Then your mom. I'll bring you out some lemonade."

She was right. He would just keep thinking about it, and they would find out from someone else. Town gossip would reach his mother. Cooper might hear something upsetting. He leaned forward. The seeds of truth would be easier to plant now so the news wouldn't be a total shock.

The boys walked to the back deck, Big Mack between them. "Mom. I want to show my treasure maps and mazes to Cooper. He draws too."

"Later. For now, come inside with me. Bridges and Cooper need to talk, and I am going to make lemonade."

The older boy stuffed his hands in the front of his hoodie and scanned the backyard. He had refused to take it off despite the warm weather. He shifted back and forth on his feet.

"Hey. Come sit down. Let's talk, just you and me, before we head to my mother's house."

"What's wrong?" He didn't sit.

"Nothing. I just want to talk to you about some of the stuff going on. It's all good. Come on. Sit."

Shoulders slumped forward, the twelve-year-old wouldn't meet his gaze.

"Cooper, you're not being sent away."

There was a nod but not a very confident one.

"I know you've been told I'm your father. That picture was taken over twelve years ago, and a lot of time has passed. I want to be up-front with everything."

Cooper glanced at him, then looked away.

Bridges took a deep breath and leaned closer. "Cooper, I was close to your age when my father died. I would have been lost without my mother and sisters. I can only imagine how alone you feel."

As much as they drove him crazy, they also gave him purpose and a place to belong. He might have carried a heavy responsibility when he'd stepped into his father's shoes, but he'd still had his family. Cooper was so alone.

In the long silence, Cooper finally made eye contact. Bridges wanted to reach out to him, but he held back. Emotions were hard. Maybe he should wait for

Lilianna. She was good at this sort of stuff. "Promise me that you'll listen to everything I have to say." He waited for a response.

"Okay."

"Good. This is hard, but I want you to know everything that's going on. I'm not judging your mother, but I'm not sure why she insisted that I was your father. I never dated her."

The boy stiffened. All the anger and resentment came flooding back into his expression.

"Cooper, please listen. I'm not going anywhere, and I'm not saying your mother lied to you with malicious intent. I just want to let you know that if we do a DNA test, it might not have the results you expect. I don't want you to be surprised or anxious."

Cooper didn't bolt, but he didn't ease back into the chair either. Sitting on the edge, fingers balled into a tight fist, he blinked several times. "Why would she lie to me?"

"When did she start telling you I was your father? Maybe her memories weren't really clear. There are some things we'll never know. If I'm not your biological father, it doesn't change you staying with me for the moment. It's easier for the system to let you stay if they believe that, so I let it stand for now." He just didn't have the heart to completely destroy the kid with the truth. He'd find a way to ease into this. Once Cooper trusted him, they would deal with total reality.

"But if you might not be my father, then why even bother with me?"

"You might not understand this, but I do believe that God put me in your path. And I was raised by a mother that gave shelter to anyone who needs it." Bridges reached out and squeezed the boy's shoulder. "I promise we're gonna get this figured out. I know people who have wrestled with addiction, just like your mother did. It's a beast some people can't fight. That doesn't mean she didn't love you, but we might not be able to trust what she thought was real."

Cooper looked away. "I want you to be my father. My mom said that you were a great guy, and that if you knew about me, you'd make it right. She wouldn't lie to me about this. She wouldn't. A lot of people think that she was a loser, but she didn't lie to me. I know drugs caused a lot of problems. She was honest about the struggle. But she was trying to get me back. She told me she was clean. The last couple of times we met, she was. She was so excited about finding you. It was all coming together, and she was happy. You have to be my father."

Bridges stood. His chest was tight from the pain he was causing the boy. What if she had discovered the truth in her search and it had pushed her over the edge?

Cooper made a strangled noise, but he had turned away from Bridges. There was a sob he couldn't hide.

"Cooper." He laid a hand on his shoulder.

With an angry grunt, Cooper shoved Bridges's hand off and ran.

Bridges stood to go after him, but he stopped at the end of the patio. This time Cooper ran to the ladder and climbed into the tree house. A safe place.

Big Mack looked up at him. "Go on. He needs someone, and he doesn't want me to see him crying." The dog barked once, then followed Cooper. He took the wall in a couple of leaps.

Bridges stood watching, waiting for any indication the boy needed him to intervene. Lilianna came through the back door with a tray of lemonade. "Where's Cooper?"

"Hiding in the tree house with Mack. He's upset that there's even a possibility that I'm not his biological father."

"I know it's hard, but you had to tell him."

"I just hope it wasn't too soon." He shook his head, then looked around. "Where's Sebastian?"

"I wasn't sure if you were ready for both of us, so I bribed him with a video game." Picking up a glass, she stepped off the deck and toward the tree. "I'm going to check on him."

"Don't." Bridges reached to stop her. "Give him space."

Turning, she tilted her head and studied him for a long minute. "To be left alone? Is that what you wanted when your father died?"

He narrowed his gaze at her. "What does that have to do with this?"

"You were about the same age Cooper is now when your world was turned upside down. What did you want?"

With a rough, gruff sound, he sat. Lilianna sat down next to him and waited for him to talk.

"What I wanted was my father not to die of cancer." Anger flashed. Why couldn't the world be fair and let kids have a childhood before tragedy forced them to grow up? He took a breath. There was no changing the past, and Lilianna had dealt with more than her fair share of heartache too. "Sorry. What I wanted then was for people to never see me cry. Ever."

She reached over and took his hand in hers. Just like she had at his father's funeral. His throat burned. Swallowing hard, he looked to the tree where Cooper was hiding. He knew what it was like to deal with the loss of a parent at a young age.

"Let me help with Cooper. I want to help you both. There are so many layers you both need to peel through. He needs to know it's healthy to cry."

"Maybe, but it's also a weakness that I didn't want to expose in front of others. Believe me, Cooper would hate for us to see him like that. When he's ready, he'll come out, and I'll take him to my mom. It'll be fine."

"And neither of you will talk about the fear of failure or the pain of loss."

"Failure is not an option. I'll make sure of that. You have to keep moving forward. That's what my father taught me." He sat back, and pain seared his shoulder. Trying to hide it from Lilianna, he bit his tongue and held still, breathing through the hurt.

She came to his side and dropped to her knees. "Bridges, what's wrong? Is it the wound?"

So much for not showing his discomfort. The pain was still too intense to speak, so he smiled at her. Pulling a deep breath through his nostrils, he relaxed.

"Bridges?" She tugged at his collar to get a better look at the injury.

He stopped her, placing his hand on top of hers. "I'm fine. I didn't get much sleep last night."

He had been worried about his mother. About getting back to work. Although it was his lack of desire to return to the force that stressed him out the most. If he didn't head home to Oklahoma, what would he do? Those worries all seemed so small compared to his new complications. A son who wasn't really his son. A woman he had always loved but couldn't have. And it was all happening in his hometown. In his mother's backyard.

"Bridges?"

"Sorry. It's just sore, nothing more." For a few minutes, they both stared at each other, her hand on his collarbone, his hand on top of hers. He needed to release her and put space between them, but he held her there.

She searched his face. Her lashes were so long. He wanted to lean forward and rest his forehead against hers, to just be close. To rest his heart.

With a jerk, he sat back. Those were the kinds of thoughts he couldn't have around her.

"Anti-inflammatories would help. Do you have any kind of painkillers?"

"Not on me."

"Hold on a minute. I'll be right back." She went into the house.

Head tilted back, he searched the sky for answers. Why had God put him here with her when he couldn't have her as his? Was he ever going to get a break?

The door opened, and Lilianna stepped in front of him with her hand out, two pills in her palm. Her other hand held a dark purple smoothie. "Take these and drink this. It's full of natural anti-inflammatories."

"Yes, Nurse Espinoza." He was enjoying the smoothie and the silence until she let out an overly heavy sigh. With one brow lifted he looked at her.

"If you don't get him I will. Giving him space is one thing, but he also needs someone that will always come for him. You had a home full of people you wanted to avoid. He's never had that."

"You're right. I'm also a little nervous. What if I say or do the wrong thing?"

"You will."

"Thanks."

She laughed. "We all do. If you wait until you have the perfect thing to say, he'll always be alone. Don't let the fear stop you from letting him know he has a home."

"How did you get so smart?"

"I'm a forever student in the school of hard knocks. Stop stalling and go get him."

"Yes, ma'am." Stopping at the base of the tree, he looked up, but he couldn't see Cooper. He hoped he wouldn't have to climb the thing. "Cooper?"

There were three heartbeats of silence, then he heard a tentative "Yes."

"Are you ready to go? Lilianna made me this really good smoothie. We could go to the store to get the ingredients to make our own. We can also pick up any of your favorite foods. Growing up, I loved cereal, but my mom didn't let me get it often. She never let me get Fruity Pebbles. They are now my guilty pleasure. Do you have a favorite?"

"I don't know." Cooper poked his head through the trapdoor, Mack right beside him. A strange sense of being here before rattled Bridges's brain for a moment.

He smiled up. "This'll be fun. Come down and we'll go to the store and buy every box of cereal you want, then we'll have a taste test. Maybe I'll find a new favorite, or we can mix them and make our own." He stepped back and waited for Cooper and Mack to come down. Then they walked to the patio.

"Sebastian's inside playing video games. Want to join him?"

"Sure." The three of them went into the house. Sebastian was excited to have Cooper man the second remote.

Lilianna sat at her kitchen table, writing on a note-pad. Bridges wasn't sure how he would cope with being around her, but he couldn't deny that she had helped him through one of the strangest days of his life. "Thank you for everything."

She looked up and smiled at him. "Call your mother while they play the game."

He'd do anything to keep her smiling. He groaned and rolled his neck back. Even call his mother to tell her he had a son that wasn't his. How did he even explain this?

Cooper darted a nervous glance over his shoulder. "Is she mean?"

Lilianna chuckled. "No. Not at all. She'll want to smother you with hugs and feed you until you pop. Bridges is just a complete coward when it comes to his mom. He's afraid of her, but she's like this tall." Lilianna held her hand right under the five-foot mark.

"She's small, but she had to keep seven kids in line. It'll be fine. She'll love you without a doubt." Bridges squinted one eye at Lilianna. "Maybe you can call her?"

"Oh no. This has to come from you."

"She's going to try to twist this to make it sound as if I have to move home."

Lilianna laughed. "She will. But you're a big boy and can tell her no. Do you need to practice?"

"No."

"See? You can do it."

They sat and chatted about people they knew and the upcoming Summerfest celebration while the boys finished a couple of games. He'd probably stalled as long as he should. She pushed him out the back door and called his mother, then went inside, leaving him alone to talk to her.

About a half hour later he came into the house. "Let's go to my mom's, then to reward ourselves, we'll go buy all the cereal boxes in the store."

Lilianna went into the living room. She sat on the chair next to Cooper and handed him a folded piece of paper. "This has my number and a list of other important ones you might need. Call me at any time of the day or night, and I will answer. Okay?"

Cooper took off his backpack and carefully placed the paper in one of the inside pockets.

Bridges frowned. "Do you have a phone?"

Head down, he shook it.

"We'll take care of that. I have an old one. We'll just get you a number and activate it. I should have thought of the list. Thanks."

"Just a part of being a mom."

How did one become a dad overnight? He was about to find out. They stood in silence. There was nothing else to say, nothing else keeping him here, but he couldn't get his feet moving to his truck.

"You're coming with us, right?" he asked.

"Afraid of facing your mother alone?"

"Having reinforcements is always solid plan. Will you come?"

"Any excuse to eat your mother's cooking. I'm in."

Grinning, he leaned in to kiss her cheek, then stopped himself. Her large eyes blinked at him in surprise. In all the years they had known each other, he had never allowed himself to slip like that. With a fast step back, he twisted away from her and moved to his truck. Distance. There had to be as much distance as possible between them.

He opened the back door, and Big Mack jumped in. Pain shot through his shoulder.

Cooper was climbing into the passenger seat. "What happened?"

"Nothing."

"I thought you said you weren't going to lie to me."

Lilianna was still standing at the backyard gate where the driveway ended. "My shoulder hurts. And I'm not sure why I got in the truck. My mother's house is within walking distance."

"Is it Lilianna? Do you like her? That can turn awkward really fast if she doesn't like you back."

Bridges laughed. Was he that obvious? Poor Lilianna. She was going to hate him.

"Go join her and Sebastian. I'll call my mom and let her know we're coming over."

Chapter Seven

Lilianna was so confused about what had just happened with Bridges. Had he been about to kiss her? It was just a peck on the cheek out of gratitude. She was tired and stressed. Her mind was running wild. It could have been anything.

As they walked to the soft coral house trimmed in white, Lilianna was swamped by a warm, comforting feeling of coming home. Even from here, she could see bright fiesta-colored plastic chairs stacked under a peach tree. Someone had been engineering a way to reach the higher branches.

She grinned at her own childhood memories.

Sebastian had skipped ahead of them.

"If this is your mom's house, why don't you stay here?" Cooper's voice was low.

"My mother wishes I did, but I like the space on a ranch."

"Sebastian said that the ranch was far away from people and town." Cooper frowned, obviously not understanding why Bridges would want to be out there alone.

Bridges chuckled. "Exactly."

"Did you know my mom and Tío Bridges were friends as kids? Along with my dad," Sebastian explained.

Cooper looked at Lilianna and frowned. "You're married?"

Sebastian squeezed himself closer to her. "My dad's dead. He was a hero in the Army. My mom, dad and Tío Bridges were all best friends when they were little. He was my dad's best friend, and now he's my best friend too."

Memories flooded Lilianna's mind as they paused outside the gate. The porch swing called to her to come sit down and take a break. Her nose burned from the bittersweet tears that wanted to fall. She had spent so many hours on that swing with Eduardo, plotting their next adventure as Bridges warned him of all the reasons they shouldn't do whatever he had dreamed up. They usually did it anyway, and Bridges made sure to bring a first-aid kit and water, just in case.

It was strange how she hadn't even known that she had needed this until she stood there. Yolanda Espinoza had filled the gap of a missing mother to a young girl who'd felt lost and alone in the world.

Now Yolanda's son was carrying on the family tradition of taking in kids who had nowhere else to go. Bridges was providing a home to a boy he had never met and had no reason to help. Why couldn't the world be filled with more people like the Espinozas?

Bridges knelt in front of Sebastian. "Cooper is new here, so I need you to introduce him to all the cousins. Can you do that?"

He stood a little taller. "I can."

Bridges stood and looked at her. "I understand why

Cooper and I are apprehensive, but I don't get why you're stalling."

"Just remembering." She lifted a shoulder, hoping to appear relaxed. "You're the one that doesn't want to go in."

The twelve-year-old took a step back. "Is it because of me? Are you worried about taking me to your family?"

Bridges moved to put his arm around the boy's shoulder. "Oh, they want you here. The only thing we should be worried about is them not letting us leave."

She was afraid that once she stepped into the little yard, she'd never want to go back to her other life.

Bridges's free hand took hers. Concern filled his deep brown eyes. "Are you okay?" They stood close together, and she took a deep breath of coastal air mixed with his masculine scent. She had missed him as much as she had missed the seashore.

With a nod, she gave him a reassuring smile.

"Then let's go in." He winked.

He grinned at her and pulled Cooper a little closer. "Welcome to the Espinoza Headquarters. I hope you like people telling you what to do, because you will get that in abundance."

"Your whole family still lives in the house you grew up in?" Cooper asked. His voice was full of wonder.

"Mostly. When my dad was alive, he managed a ranch outside of town. So, we stayed out there most of the time, but then he bought this. It was a tiny, one-room house, and he added each extra room on himself. It's five times bigger now. During the school year, we split our time between the two until his death. Then we moved here permanently. I left for the Army at eighteen, then moved to Oklahoma when I got out."

"If I had a real home, I'd never leave. I'm glad you were here so I could find you."

"Me too."

Smoothing out his T-shirt, Bridges was wanting everyone to think he had it under control, but she knew him, and he was battling self-doubt. About what, she wasn't sure.

Sebastian was ready to go in. "Yesterday was my first time visiting here. They've always come to San Antonio to see us. My mom grew up here, but I didn't. Where'd you grow up?"

"Around." Cooper shrugged.

Lilianna locked her arm with Bridges's and led him through the gate. "Come on, guys. There are people peeking out the window wondering why we're not coming in. Let's stop the torture. They want to meet the newest Espinoza."

Cooper froze, his heels planted. "They're okay with me showing up out of nowhere saying I'm your son?"

Bridges hugged Cooper's shoulders. "I promise it's okay. My mom knows you're coming. She knows about you hiding in town looking for me and us meeting you at the police station. I told her that you lost your mom and that you need a place to stay. To be honest, she probably told all my siblings. I should warn you—I have six. Which means that pretty much everyone knows, and they can't wait to meet you. *Familia* is everything to them, and you are part of that now."

"You have six brothers and sisters?" Cooper's mouth dropped open.

"Just one brother. Five sisters."

Sebastian opened the gate. "Nica and Josh's *abuelita*

said we could have peach cobbler today from the ones we picked yesterday."

The door swung open, and Yolanda Espinoza walked to the edge of the front porch. She was under five feet tall. Her silver hair was thick and cut in a short, angled line, making her look like a wise pixie who could relay the truths of the universe, if a person was willing to sit still and listen. "Why are y'all standing out here in the heat when I've got *carne guisada* in the kitchen waiting to be eaten?" She wiped her hands on her apron, then waved them toward the bright red door. "Come in. Come in. This must be Cooper. Such a handsome young man. Come in and meet everyone."

Everyone? Lilianna sent a worried glance to Bridges. For Yolanda, that could be up to twenty people.

"Mom, who's here? I told you to keep this first meeting small and quiet." Bridges guided Cooper into the house. "Don't let them intimidate you. I promise they have the best intentions, but they can act like a huge litter of Labrador puppies. In their eagerness to greet you, they lose all self-control and end up covering you in slobber and dirt."

Cooper's eyes went wide. Lilianna shook her head. "He's just teasing you. They're good people, I promise. And yes, they are a little eager to bring newbies into the fold. I've heard Mrs. Espinoza say 'the more the merrier' a few hundred times."

Bridges had one hand resting on Cooper's bony shoulder. Her heart went out to the man. There was an air of loneliness around him. Even in the large chaos of his family, he had always stood a little to the side, a part of them but alone at the same time.

She never had figured that out about him. But she had

Sebastian—and now Cooper—to worry about. Bridges was a grown adult who could obviously take care of himself, and he was living the life he wanted.

Bridges fell in step behind Lilianna and the two boys. She was a natural caregiver. How did she always know what people wanted before they did?

Sebastian held on tight to his mother. Then he leaned across her to get closer to Cooper. "She's super nice, and she likes feeding people." He led them in as if it were his home.

Yolanda swept Cooper into a hug. Her energy and love made her ten times bigger than her small frame. "Oh, *mijo*. I'm so happy you found us." Tears welled in her eyes.

"Mom." Bridges stepped in and put his hand on her arm, gently releasing the death grip she had on Cooper. She made his five-ten feel much taller. "Please. Don't overwhelm him."

"Oh, silly." She swatted his arm. "Everyone needs a good hug, and I am glad he's here. He needs to know that."

She headed to the back of the house, leaving them alone in the living room. Savory scents filled the air. Bridges could see through to the kitchen. Two of his sisters were there. Marguerite was standing at the stove, heating up tortillas.

Savannah, the sister two years younger than him was chopping cucumbers. Leaving her chore behind, she gave him a gentle hug. As a midwife in San Antonio, she'd spent the most time with Lilianna. "Mom has been harassing me to check on you. She's worried about your recovery."

He rolled his eyes. "Not a lot of gunshot wounds in your line of work." He turned to his only brother. Reno, the youngest of the siblings, sat eating at the table. He was home from college. With a huge grin, Reno stood and gave him a tight hug that included heavy thumping on his back. Bridges tried to hold back the wince.

"Oh, sorry. I forgot about the shoulder."

"I'm good."

"Introduce me to this guy right here." He put out his hand to Cooper, then pulled him into a hug. His family had no clue about personal space.

"So glad you're here." He winked at Bridges. "You're gonna be glad too, once you get a taste of this *carne guisada*."

Four kids rushed in from the hallway, followed by his mother. A chorus of "Tío Bridges!" warmed his heart. He loved his nieces and nephew. Not seeing them more was a huge drawback to not living closer.

"It's the *mocosos pequeños*." Bridges laughed as they rushed him with hugs.

"I'm not a little brat anymore." Angie, the oldest of the grandkids, said as she stepped back.

"Yes. I see you have become *mocasa grande*." He rubbed the top of her head. She was looking more like her mother every day. The other kids laughed.

"She's the biggest brat of all," her sister, Nica, joked.

Angie glared at her with her arms crossed.

"Okay, guys. Be nice. Sebastian, why don't you introduce Cooper to the *primos*?"

The cousins turned as one to Cooper, eyeing him with open curiosity, but they all became very polite.

"Cooper, this is Angie, the oldest. She's eleven. Then her sister, Nica, is eight. There's Josh. He's six. Desirae is seven like me." He pointed to a redhead with green eyes. "Her mom, Tía Josefina, is not here. *Primos*, this is Cooper. He's twelve."

The kids just stared at each other for a bit. Bridges was about to say something—*anything*—when Angie raised her hand.

Not sure if he should give the inquisitive preteen the floor, he hesitated before nodding to her.

Angie looked between them all. "Is it true that you didn't know you had a son? How does this happen? And does this mean I'm not the oldest grandchild anymore?"

"I am his son." Cooper stiffened and took a step back, bumping into him. "I am." Panic edged his voice.

Bridges placed a hand on his shoulder. "It's okay Cooper." He thought his sisters and mother would have the hard questions. He forgot never to underestimate kids. He had no idea what to say.

Lilianna joined him, her arm brushing his.

She smiled at the kids. "This is a wonderful surprise, and you have someone new to play with."

With his hand still on Cooper, Bridges reached out and pulled Angie against him. It hadn't even occurred to him that she would have a problem with the new cousin taking her place. "Hey, *mocosa*. It's complicated, but the important thing is that he's here with me now. The Espinozas stick together no matter what, right?"

She nodded.

"He's part of the *familia*, so be nice."

"But she's not nice to us, and we're *familia* too." Josh pouted.

"I am too. I'm very nice when you're not ruining my things."

Marguerite set a bowl full of *carne guisada* on the

table, along with a basket of tortillas. She put her arm around her oldest daughter. "We talked about this. Being the oldest means you have more understanding of life and need to be a leader. Did y'all finish organizing the playroom?"

"No, ma'am."

"Okay. You have met Cooper. Now, go finish your jobs and check the chickens." She kissed the top of her daughter's head. "Hurry. You have things to do, then you can get to know Cooper and show him around. But for the time being, out of the kitchen." The children disappeared down the hallway.

"Cooper, sit down and eat. Don't worry about the kids. It's summer and they're bored. Maybe later we can all go to the beach and you can get to know them better. They were very excited about meeting you."

Cooper looked at Bridges. The boy had the look of a wild animal about to bolt, but Marguerite went on, ignoring his hesitation. "Now that Lilianna is back in town, we'll have to get all the kids together."

The poor kid's eyes went wide. "There's more?"

Bridges cleared his throat. "I think we want to take it slow. The plan for today is to have lunch with y'all and meet the kids. Then chill at the cabin and get Cooper settled. This is a lot to take in, and I think he needs rest." He looked at Cooper. "What do you think? Just a day hanging out at my place, getting settled in?"

Cooper shoved a spoonful of *carne guisada* into his mouth and nodded.

Bridges's mother rested her hand on her chest. "Look at you, being all fatherly." Tears stood in her eyes again.

Marguerite put more food on the table. "Mother

would love for you to be here. The kids are at the house all the time."

Reno laughed. "Don't let the sisters railroad you." He handed Cooper a tortilla. "But you have to use one of her tortillas to eat that."

Savannah handed him a plate with the radish-and-cucumber salad and sat next to Lilianna.

Marguerite put her hands on her hips and glared at them as Bridges went to fill his own bowl. He sat next to Cooper, across from Reno. His baby brother was smirking at him like he knew something that Bridges didn't.

Marguerite pulled out the heavy wooden chair at the head of the table and sat. Yolanda was at the other end. "Mom and I have been talking."

Bridges wanted to groan and slam his head on the tabletop. Lilianna nudged his foot. He forced a smile and waited for his sister to plan his life.

"Now that you have custody of Cooper, we think it would be better for you to move back into the house. Your bedroom is ready for you, and there's an extra room for Cooper. This way we can make sure that you're both taken care of. With your injury, you need to be careful not to overdo it. I've read up on this sort of thing, and if you're not careful, there can be permanent damage. More importantly, Cooper needs family. He's a growing boy and needs plenty of good, cooked food."

"And here I was, going to feed him bad, uncooked food."

She ignored him and turned to Lilianna and Savannah. "Lilianna, you're a nurse. Don't you agree that it's too soon for him to be out on his own? And now, with Cooper? It's too much, right?"

Lilianna stuffed a big bite of tortilla full of meat and

gravy into her mouth, and her eyes went wide. His sister wasn't going to let her off that easy, though. Bridges sat back and crossed his arms. Hands peacefully folded in front of her, Marguerite waited for Lilianna to finish eating.

Realizing she wasn't going to avoid this, Lilianna sighed. "Bridges says that he can take care of himself. In my professional opinion, he can. He knows his limits. Plus, we're down the road from the ranch. He passes us on his way into town. I can go out and check on him if that makes you feel better. But I don't think he needs to move back home."

"Not that you asked me," Savannah said as she added more salad to her plate, "but I agree with Lilianna."

Yolanda made a disgruntled sound, obviously unhappy that they had not backed up their plans for Bridges and Cooper. "But poor Cooper needs our full attention, and Bridges is just being *obstinato*. He was shot." She covered her mouth with her hand. "Why do you have to be so bullheaded?"

Oh no. Not the tears. The victory Bridges had silently been celebrating faded. He couldn't handle his mother crying. It made him feel like the kid who'd been unable to do anything to fix her pain after his father's death.

"Momma. Please."

Her lips trembled. "When a mother gets a call that her oldest boy was shot in the line of duty... I just can't."

"Mom. I'm okay. I'm right here. The ranch is not that far." He took her free hand and rubbed it with his thumb. "This is not about me being stubborn, I promise. I'm thirty-one years old. I need my own space. Cooper and I need time to get to know each other."

"But who better to take care of you than your mother?" His sister wasn't going to let it go.

Words would be a waste of air, so he tried glaring her down. It didn't faze her.

"Bridges." She glared right back. "Cooper needs to get to know his grandmother and family. With Lilianna and Sebastian just a few houses away for the first time, it's like you're meant to be home."

"Mom. Nothing has been settled yet. He might have another family out there. Besides, I am home. Just right down the road. You'll probably see us every day. Let it go. We're staying at the cabin." He shoved the bowl across the table. The motion yanked at his wound. He bit down to hide the sharp pain. Seeing his distress would totally defeat his insistence that he didn't need them.

Sebastian ran in from the back room, unaware of the tension building between the adults. "We're going to check the chickens. Does Cooper want to come? I've never seen real chickens before. Angie said we might find eggs."

Cooper, who had gone very still during the conversation, glanced at Bridges. "Is it okay?"

"If you want to go, sure. Watch out for the red rooster. He's got an attitude, and it's not good."

Cooper stood up, his bowl in hand. "Thank you for the *carne guisada*." He stumbled over the words. "It was really good. Where do you want me to put this?"

Yolanda stood. "Oh, what a sweet boy." She cupped his face, then took the bowl. "Here. I'll take that and wash it for you. Go with the children. Get to know your *primos*."

"*Gracias*."

"*De nada. De nada.*" She smiled at Bridges as the

boys left. "That boy has good manners. He's an Espinoza. I can tell."

"Mom." He glanced over his shoulder and waited for all the little ears to be gone before continuing, "I told you that, more than likely, he is not my biological son. What I should have told you is that there is no way he's mine, but he doesn't know that. It's too soon."

"All children need a home and family. Stability." Marguerite clicked her tongue as she cleared the table. "Just sign the papers or whatever it is you need to do to make sure he is safe."

"I'm not going to rush this without knowing the truth. What if he has a father who wants him?" Bridges shook his head. "I can't do that. A lie that big can cause tons of damage."

"It's for his own good. Will telling him the truth help or hurt?" His mother added to the argument.

Bridges sighed. He glanced at his baby brother. "I'm sure you have an opinion on this too."

Reno held up his hands. "Not me. You have plenty of voices. I'm sure you know what you want to do. I'd go with that." He glanced at his phone. "There's a game on TV I planned to watch. Want to join me while we wait for the peach cobbler?"

"Sure." His brother had always had the talent of avoiding any confrontation with his mother and sisters. "As soon as we eat the cobbler, Cooper and I are leaving."

"Does Cooper want to leave?" his sister asked.

He gave his sister his sternest glare. She just rolled her eyes and went to the kitchen, grabbing Lilianna's arm and drawing her along.

He really just wanted to unplug and not think. Did his

family think he was incapable of taking care of a kid? They acted as if he was making some huge mistake not moving into his mother's home.

He probably was.

He sighed. The one thing he knew for sure was that, if it all went wrong, they would be there for him. His family might push him to the edge of his limits, but they would catch him if he fell.

Making sure they wouldn't be forced to hold him up was the problem he faced. It was his job to take care of them. His father had made sure he understood that before he died. He was the man of the family, and their happiness and safety were his responsibility.

The kids came in, excited to show him the different colored eggs they had found. The cobbler was pulled out of the oven and ice cream was scooped on top.

Reno lost control of the TV and went to his room out back to finish watching the game. Bridges stood and hugged his mother. "I love you. Cooper and I need to go into town."

"Are you sure you don't want to stay here?"

He kissed her on top of her silver head. "I'm sure."

"Well, listen to Lilianna. She is a nurse and a mother. She's always been a smart girl."

"Yes, ma'am."

"I'm with you." Lilianna stood up from the table. "Let's get the boys, and I'll follow you."

His mother followed him through the kitchen. "If you lived here, you wouldn't have anywhere to go. You'd already be home."

He kissed her on the forehead. "Mom, please let it go. I'm not moving back into your house. If you keep after me, I'm heading to Oklahoma sooner than planned."

She gasped. "You can't do that."

He raised a brow. "I don't want to turn every visit into a battle of wills. It would be easier for all of us if I didn't come around."

"No. I've said my piece. I won't bring it up again. But you know your old room is always ready for you."

"Thank you." He pressed his hand to his chest. "Just knowing you are here for me makes getting through the day easier."

With a nod, she let him go.

Outside, the sun was high in the clear blue sky. Not a single cloud spotted the horizon. After another restless night, his shoulder was hurting, but he didn't want his favorite nurse to notice. Keeping his distance was the best course of action. The boys were chatting about the cousins. She looked over her shoulder at him and smiled.

His mind took a snapshot of her golden skin shining in the sun, her face open and full of joy. His gut twisted. She was so beautiful. Not just her looks, but the glow in her eyes made life brighter.

The boys challenged her to a race. Laughing, they took off, Big Mack running with them. That was his family. The one he'd never have.

She was Eduardo's. He was just feeling lost because of the shotgun wound. He was pushing himself to get better, to reach the point where they would release him to go back to work. But going back to Oklahoma didn't settle right in his gut. If he wasn't a police officer, what was he?

Chapter Eight

"What's a cattle guard?" They had been in Port Del Mar a week now. Sebastian strained against his seat belt as he took in the surrounding ranch. Lilianna's little car was designed for city roads, not potholes and bouncing over large pipes.

"They dig a hole in the road, then put metal bars over it. Trucks and cars can travel over them, but it keeps the cattle in the right pasture."

"How deep is the hole?"

"Um… I don't know. We'll have to come back and measure it."

"Is there water or spikes in the hole? I could use it as an obstacle in one of my mazes. That would be cool. Is that Tío Bridges's house?" His hands were pressed against the window. "It looks like it's from the Old West movie I watched with Grandpa."

Putting the car in Park, she smiled. "It does."

The cabin wasn't big, but it had a deep front porch that covered the entire front. "I can see why Bridges loves it out here. He always said he wished he'd been born when the vaqueros ruled the land."

"What's a vaquero?"

She needed to speak more Spanish with him. The Espinozas could help with that. "Vaqueros are the original cowboys from Mexico. A lot of the terms and skills that cowboys use came from them."

"I want to be a vaquero!"

"I thought you wanted to be a policeman." She smiled. What he wanted to be changed just about every seven days. She gathered the bags that contained the casserole and the ingredients for a salad.

This was their first trip to the ranch, but they had had several meals with Bridges and Cooper every day for a week now. The boys were bonding. Sebastian had told her it was cool to be around someone who didn't look at him with a sad face. That's what people did at school and church. He smiled, saying that Cooper understood, and that they could talk about their dead parents without it getting weird.

Her heart swelled for Cooper. She prayed for him and thanked God for bringing him into their lives.

Twice this week, they had met at the Espinoza family's bakery shop, Panaderia de Dulces, so that she could keep Cooper while Bridges went to physical therapy. The routine had been so easy to slip into. She missed being part of a family.

But something was off with Bridges. Conversations used to flow between them with little effort, whereas now it seemed as if he didn't want to make eye contact. Her friend was slipping away, and she didn't know why.

Today she'd talk to him. She'd never been nervous around him before, but as they walked to the cabins, butterflies leaped and swirled.

"This is like a real ranch." Sebastian took in the sprawling land, the barns and the two cabins.

"It is a real ranch. Just like the one your dad and Bridges worked on as kids. Your grandfather and father were ranch hands on another spread."

"I thought he was an Army hero." He followed her up the steps to the front door of the cabin.

"He was, but we are more than one thing in life. Like Bridges. He worked on the ranch. Then he went into the Army, and now he's a police officer."

"I can be in the Army, be a police officer and a vaquero, and I can make roller coasters."

"Engineers design roller coasters. That would be such a cool job." Her mother's heart might not survive him joining the Army or becoming a law enforcer.

She knocked on the door. After a few minutes of silence, she tried the handle. The door opened. Stepping inside, she could see straight to the back door. The living room, dining room and kitchen formed one big, open space. There was a small sofa with a coffee table, and a couple of bar stools stood at a small island. There were a few dishes in the sink, but other than that, it barely looked lived in. A universal weight set and a few other pieces of exercise equipment took up the dining space.

Setting the bags on the counter, she spotted a note. The handwriting was clean and crisp. Each letter stood straight with sharp edges. "He says they're in the back, working with the dogs."

Sebastian stood at the rear door. "I see them." He charged out the back.

He was halfway across the field by the time she stepped off the porch. Past a huge garden snuggled between the two cabins, Cooper stood with Damian De La Rosa.

They were intent on the action taking place at the other end of the pasture. It looked as if Bridges was running around an obstacle course, holding something out as a black lab followed him.

She hadn't seen Damian since she'd left Port Del Mar. He'd been a few years younger, and her father hadn't wanted her hanging around the De La Rosa family back then. Like Eduardo and Bridges, Damian had joined the military right after school, and the three men had become close friends.

Looking at Damian from here, she couldn't even tell he had any injuries, but she knew that he'd lost his left arm and leg during his service overseas. It had happened about a year before she'd lost Eduardo. He'd gone to visit Damian in the hospital. She should have been better about keeping in touch.

Yolanda and Marguerite had filled her in on all the De La Rosa drama. Damian was now married and running the ranch with his cousin Belle. Maybe he was the perfect person for Bridges to be around right now.

Bridges liked to pretend he had it all together, but there was no way that he wasn't affected by having been shot.

Damian called out words of encouragement as Bridges and the dog sprinted toward them. Big Mack saw them first and barked a greeting. The two big dogs on either side of Damian turned with him. She called out to Sebastian. That pair looked as if they could take down a grown man without any effort.

Cooper ran toward them, Mack on his heels.

Sebastian bounced in excitement.

"Careful. We don't know the other dogs." She'd seen too many kids in the emergency room with wounds from bites.

"Oh, it's okay. They look mean. But Hansel and Gretel are the best dogs. I mean, not as cool as Big Mack here, but they are super sweet."

Damian joined them. Holding out his hand to her, he gave her an earnest smile. "Hi, Lilianna. It's been a long time. I'm so sorry to hear about Eduardo. I would have been at the memorial, but…" Guilt clouded his green-gray eyes.

"Don't apologize. You were doing what you needed to do. Thank you for the letter and the picture. They meant a lot to me. You look good."

Bridges came up behind him and patted him on the shoulder. "I told Damian you would find us in record time."

Damian laughed. "Most people only get here by accident. We're way off the GPS grid."

"Lilianna has always had the best sense of direction. She saved Eduardo and me from our adolescent stupidity a couple of times."

"Well, you are always welcome on the ranch. If there is anything I can do for you or Sebastian, let me know. Have you moved back to town permanently? Eduardo was always talking about moving back."

She tried not to react, but that startled her. Eduardo had never told her he wanted to move back to Port Del Mar. "No. We're just here for the summer."

"Is that a maze?" Sebastian asked Bridges, pointing to where the dogs had been.

"It's actually an obstacle course that's used for training."

Cooper nodded. "Bridges said I can help. Damian's teaching dogs to find people that are hurt or lost. He trains horses too."

"I want to help."

"Hey, Sebastian." Damian bent down a little and held out his hand to shake.

"How do you know my name?"

"I'd recognize you anywhere. You look just like your father. We grew up together here in Port Del Mar."

Bridges joined them. "Cooper was about to run the course with Gretel. She's a pro. Want to go with them? You can shadow Cooper."

Her son looked to Cooper. "Can I? That would be so cool." He vibrated with more excitement than she had seen in the last few months. Maybe Cooper having even a bigger impact on her little family as they were helped him. She kept her arms tight around her waist so that she wouldn't reach out and hug the boys to her.

"Sure. Stay on my left. Gretel will be on my right."

Damian gave the boys instructions. "Make sure to use the hand signals. She's deaf." He took them to the start of the course.

Bridges moved next to her. "The boys are getting along so well. I think they're helping each other deal with the mess life has given them."

She nodded. She had come home to Port Del Mar for her son's well-being, but Bridges and Cooper were an unexpected bonus. Why had she fought returning? She should have learned by now to trust God. In just the short time she had known Cooper, she had come to care for him in a fierce, protective motherly manner.

This was where they needed to be, and God knew

it. Bridges needed her, even if he didn't admit it. "How are you today?"

"I'm solid. I'm going to help Damian build kennels on the north side of the barn. I miss working outdoors. Funny. While I worked on the ranch with my dad, all I wanted was to get away. Now I can't remember why."

He'd done a good job of sidestepping her question.

"As kids, we're so ready to get out and live our lives, but then the reality of life hits us. We realize the value of the things that we claimed were suffocating us." She turned to him with a stern gaze. "That being said, be careful. You're not fully healed. You don't want to have another surgery."

"I can't just sit around doing nothing. I need some sort of purpose."

"You just became a foster father to a troubled preteen. How much more purpose do you want?"

He laughed so loudly that the small group on the obstacle course turned to them. He waved. "Man, when I told God I needed something to give my life meaning, He jumped right on that." He sighed. "I'm best at solving problems when I'm physically taking action. I also think it will help Cooper."

"Maybe this is your opportunity to be still and listen?"

He looked at her as if she had suddenly caught a fly with her tongue. *Gross.* Her son's obsession with frogs had invaded her mind again.

Bridges reminded her of a man doing hard penance. He denied it, but he needed her as much as the boys did. *God, is it possible to find healing for all three of these males?*

Her son was her heart, but the other two had snuck

in and taken a bit for themselves. It was already broken. What would carry it to the point that she couldn't survive? How many ways can a heart fracture? She really didn't want to learn its limits.

Bridges looked away from Lilianna. He couldn't let her see too much. If she got close enough, she'd see the cracks he was barely keeping patched. "Let's go check out the boys."

Holding his arm to guide her, they made their way across the lush grass of the cut pasture. At the start of the obstacle course, they watched as Damian walked the boys through the structures, taking the time to explain the how and why of each one.

The boys and dogs hung on each word. "He's really good at this."

"One of the best. People across the country send him horses that no one else can work with."

"You always had a gift with animals. Remember the strays you would bring home and train? Taco was my favorite."

He laughed. "Eduardo said we had to name them after the last food we ate before we found them. We had Bean, Cookie, and my favorite, Brisket."

The little group went through the last obstacle and made their way to Bridges and Lilianna. Damian smiled at them. "I think these guys are ready." He gestured to the beginning of the obstacle course. "Remember, she can't hear you, so keep your hand signals clear. Go get ready, and I'll tell you when to start."

Lilianna looked at the dogs and then to Bridges before turning to Damian. "They're going alone with her? Is it safe?"

He nodded. "I'll be right here. But they're going to take Gretel. She's a great dog. She's actually training them. These boys—" he waved toward his other two dogs "—will stay out of the way, right?" They both lay down and rested their muzzles on their front paws, looking up at him with the saddest eyes.

"Aw! They want to go, don't they?"

"They've been working all morning." He gave them each a treat, then straightened. "Okay, go."

The boys jogged along on the side as Gretel jumped the flipped barrels, then turned and ran through them. Bridges smiled as Sebastian observed Cooper closely, then copied him.

After watching the boys for a while, Lilianna studied the garden. It was large and so green.

Damian kept his gaze on the trio as Gretel jumped, climbed and crawled. "My wife tends the garden, but she's out of town right now, so there should be a lot of squash and tomatoes that you can pull if you want."

"Thank you."

Bridges tried to keep his attention on the boys, but Lilianna moved so naturally across the land that he wanted to follow. There was a wooden basket hanging on the gate. Going into the garden, she walked through the plants.

"You're hung up on your cousin's widow?" Damian asked.

"What? No." He turned his back to her and focused on the boys.

"If you're going to deny it, you'll need to learn to hide that yearning expression."

He frowned, not saying anything. He'd just sound defensive.

Sebastian ran back to them. "We did it. Can we do it again?"

Out of breath, Cooper rubbed Gretel's shoulder. "Can we? It was so fun."

The boys talked on top of each other. Damian laughed. "Sure. This time, start at the other end."

The boys ran off with Gretel on their heels. They stopped and looked at Damian, waiting for him to tell them when to go.

Standing in silence, Damian and Bridges watched Gretel leap over a short wall. Bridges' skin tightened as he fought the urge to turn around and look for Lilianna.

"Are you sure that kid isn't yours?" Earlier today, Bridges had explained the whole story to Damian and asked for his advice, so the other man knew that Cooper wasn't his.

"I'm absolutely positive."

He gestured his chin to the boys. "It's not obvious, but he moves like you."

Bridges narrowed his eyes and intently watched the boy. Cooper was staring at the dogs. So focused. His expression looked just like… "He's not mine. He can't be."

"What about your cousin? Y'all were in Georgia at the same time." He glanced over his shoulder. "She doesn't see it? The kid's twelve. Were they already married?"

"No, but they were serious." There were several times that he had been frustrated and mad at his cousin's stupidity, but what hit him just now was on a new level. Dread filled his gut.

"Oh man. Are you going to tell her that Sebastian has a brother?"

"We don't know that for sure." But everything in him

said it was true. "Why would Cooper's mother tell him I was his father?"

"Would Eduardo have given her your name?" Damian shrugged. "If he was feeling guilty, maybe he lied to her. Or she just got you confused. You both have the same look."

Heat flared from his core. His hand fisted. If Eduardo was here, he'd hit him in the face. He would have never believed in a million years that Eduardo would have cheated on Lilianna, but… He glanced at the boy. How had they missed it?

"Man. You're turning red. You might want to turn it down a notch before they notice."

Bridges took a deep breath. Eduardo wasn't here, so wanting to beat him was a waste of time and energy. "First I have to figure out if he is Eduardo's. We're just going on assumptions here."

Damian snorted.

Choosing to ignore him, Bridges went through the scenario. "There is a picture of the three of us. But I don't remember meeting her." Had she mistakenly called Eduardo Bridges and his cousin had let it stand? "Eduardo was impulsive and didn't think about the consequences, but he never ran from them. Cooper's mom said we had left before she found out, so she never told me or Eduardo." He turned his gaze to the boys on the course. They were so intent on what they were doing, their expressions identical.

How had he not seen it? But then again, maybe he had. Avoiding it was easier than upsetting the people he cared about.

He wanted the people in his world to be happy. There was no way this wouldn't shake Lilianna's foundation and alter Sebastian's image of his father as a war hero. Their world was going to crumble.

"You know—" Damian pulled Bridges out of his doomsday thoughts "—God is pretty amazing. That boy needs a family. His real family was here, ready for him. You live hundreds of miles away, and Lilianna gets the urge to come home after being gone for over a decade. You're together when you get the call to come pick up Cooper. How could this not be a God thing?"

Yay. The unspoken word was so dry it scratched his brain. Now if God would just give him the best way to tell Lilianna he suspected that her husband had another son. How did he tell Lilianna this truth without destroying Eduardo's memory?

Eduardo had made him promise that if anything happened to him while he was serving, Bridges would step up and take care of his family. Of course, Eduardo never knew that Bridges had loved Lilianna first. Between his broken promise and his guilt, he'd been a lousy friend.

There was no way Eduardo had known about Cooper. He'd never leave his kid behind. Just this morning, he'd been trying to figure out ways to spend less time with Lilianna. Ways that would keep him close to Sebastian but keep her at arm's length.

His mother always said that God laughed at the plans made by man. Great. God had a sense of humor.

Both boys needed him, and with this news, Lilianna would too. He couldn't leave her alone to deal with this revelation.

Chapter Nine

Lilianna followed Bridges and the boys to his cabin. She'd never seen her son or Cooper so animated. She knew the research behind animal therapy, but she had never seen it in action. Working together with the dogs was building the boys' confidence in a way she hadn't expected. When they had first arrived, even Bridges had seemed happier, more open.

She glanced at him. There was a storm brewing in his eyes now that had not been there earlier. Every time she tried to talk to him, he moved away from her, interacting with the boys, pretending he didn't hear her.

Bridges opened the back door. "Welcome to our home, Sebastian." He smiled as they charged past him. Cooper brightened and looked at Bridges as if he held the keys to all the rooms the preteen wanted to get into. Even with his grumpy, mad-at-the-world attitude, he couldn't hide what it meant to be included in having a home.

Lilianna put her arm around Cooper. The compulsion to hug him closer and protect him from all hurts was too strong to deny. He was too young to lose his childhood. She knew he wasn't ready for a full-on smothering of motherly love from her, but it was hard to fight.

Stepping back, she gave him some space. "It's beautiful out here. How are you liking it, Cooper?"

"It's so far out in the country. I've never seen anything like it. It's the best place I've ever lived. I've only lived in the city. Mostly apartments, until I was with my last family, but those houses were so close together there wasn't even a yard." He looked into the basket she placed on the counter.

"This place has a lot more yard than house. And food right out the back door. I never imagined there were so many noises this far away from people. I always thought it would be quiet. It's strange, though, how much I really like it."

He pointed to a wide ladder that went to the loft above. "My room's up there."

Eyes wide, Sebastian stared up with awe as the older boy started climbing. "Cool. It's like you live in a tree house."

Standing at the sink with his back to Lilianna, Bridges chuckled. "But with indoor plumbing."

Halfway up the ladder, Cooper turned to Sebastian. "Do you want to see it?" Big Mack climbed the slanted ladder, his gaze staying on Cooper.

"Make sure to wash your hands," Bridges reminded them.

"Oh no." Sebastian froze. "I forgot my notebook in the car. Could you get it for me, please? I want to draw out my ideas for a new maze design before I forget."

"You've had a lot of great inspiration today." She moved to the sink to wash her hands. Standing next to Bridges, she tried to make eye contact again.

Bridges studied his hands as he dried them, then moved to the other side of the counter. He took the casserole she'd brought and slid it into the oven.

"I don't hear the water running," he shouted to the loft. "Use that indoor plumbing and wash your hands before you do anything else."

Okay, so he wasn't going to talk to her. Skipping down the steps to the car, she searched her brain for anything she might have done to upset him. Grabbing Sebastian's backpack, she shook that thought off.

Why did women assume it was their fault when a man went all silent? Something was up with him, but there was a lot going on in his life. Growing up, he'd tended to keep his thoughts and concerns close to him.

They were friends. Why couldn't he get over himself and admit that she could help him? Slinging the backpack over her shoulder, she marched back into his cabin. "Sebastian."

Her son poked his head over the side of the loft. "Thanks, Mom. Can you toss it up?" He held out his hands and caught it easily.

"Whoa. Good throw, Ms. Espinoza."

"Please call me Lilianna, Cooper. We're family." The boys vanished back into the loft to discuss the obstacle course.

With Sebastian and Cooper occupied, she turned to Bridges. "Spill. Tell me what's wrong."

He gave her a weak smile. "Nothing. Shoulder's a little sore from yesterday's PT." He went to the refrigerator and pulled out a Dr. Pepper. "Want one?"

"No, but water would be good." She pulled out a bar stool. "Here. Sit. Let me look at it. Have you iced it?"

"This morning," he grumbled.

"Tell me what's going on." She moved to check his wound, and he slipped past her to the other side of the counter. "Okay. You've been distant this week, but today, since the obstacle course, something has you upset."

"You don't know me as well as you think you do."

"I've known you since first grade." Determined to look at his shoulder, she followed him. He sat on the bar stool and sighed, finally letting her examine his injury. She manipulated his arm and lightly massaged the area. "And I was married to your cousin. I know your family."

"He was my second cousin."

"Okay, now I know something's up. You never called each other second cousins. What is going on? You were best friends. I know you. You're on edge. Please tell me. I want to help."

"I'm just tired, and I have a few problems I need to figure out."

"Then talk to me. Sometimes hearing the problem out loud helps you work through it."

She rotated his arm again and massaged his good shoulder. "You're overcompensating on your good side, and it's throwing you out of whack. Have they given you exercises to balance the use of your shoulders? They're so tight."

With a deep sigh, he rolled his head to the left. "That feels good."

"You're a knotted ball of tension. Talk to me. We used to discuss everything. When Eduardo was gone, you'd call me and let me vent and ramble until I solved whatever problem I was dealing with at the time. Let me do that for you."

"You already have too much on your plate. It's not anything you can help me with."

"I would never—" The timer buzzed on the stove. She pointed a finger at him and narrowed her eyes. "Don't think this means you're off the hook." Pulling the casserole from the oven, she called for Sebastian and Cooper to join them.

Bridges went to the cabinet for dishes. "Come on down, guys," he yelled after the table was set, but there was still no sign of the kids.

She went to the ladder. "Cooper. Sebastian? What are you doing? It's time to eat."

"But Mom. We're working! We have the coolest ideas and Cooper is really smart."

"Bring your stuff here and show us what you're doing, but you're coming down to eat. Now."

"Yes, ma'am."

Bridges disappeared outside, then came back with two of the porch chairs. "Sorry. This place was not designed with company in mind." He pulled the small table away from the wall and added the chairs.

The three males sat as she served the cheesy enchiladas. Sebastian grinned. "These are my favorites."

Sounds of fork scrapping plates filled the silence as they ate. Her heart turned to mush. Growing up, the only thing she had ever wanted was a family. Eduardo had offered that to her, then he'd taken off on one mission after another. Until the last time, when he never came back.

He'd not ever stayed in one place long, but the days he'd been home when they'd hung out like this had been the best ever. With his death, not only had she lost her husband but she had lost the future she had wanted with him.

She had imagined at least four children and a couple of dogs. This moment brought back all those dreams and desires. But it was Bridges who sat here rekindling all those feelings she thought she had buried with Eduardo.

The problem was that Bridges made it clear that he thought of her as a sister or as his cousin's wife. He couldn't see her as anything more. Her eyes burned.

No. No. No. She would not, could not, have an emotional breakdown in front of them. Pushing away from the table, she went to the sink to refill her glass with water. "Can I get you anything while I'm up?" she offered.

"I'm finished, Mom." His plate clean, Sebastian opened his notebook. "You have to see the new designs we came up with."

"Since we're on a ranch—" Cooper's eyes glowed "—do they have hay bales or other stuff we could build this with?"

Bridges scooted closer to her so that he could see the drawings. It was the first time in the last few days he had willingly moved near her. He studied the designs.

At first, Lilianna knew he was just being supportive, but then he shifted and asked a few questions. He looked up at her. "How long has he been doing these? They're really good."

She nodded. "He started at about four. It was really crazy the way he could organize space at such a young age. He asked me to help him research real mazes, and we traveled to any that were in our area. From there, he's gotten even better." She leaned over. "What did they come up with together?"

There were three complete drawings plus a few rough sketches and several drafts. "Wow. These are great. Would they be able to use hay bales? He's built some models with Legos and stuff from my kitchen, but we've never tried to make one life-size. It never occurred to me that it was even possible."

"I have an idea. Let me make a phone call." He stood and walked out the front door. They all watched him as he paced on the porch.

"Who do you think he's talking to?" Sebastian asked.

Cooper pointed out the back. "Maybe he knows someone that has the stuff so that we can build it out here. Damian could use it for training the dogs."

"He could." Eagerness filled Sebastian's voice. "We could add false items that would help them stay focused."

The boys got all excited again and brainstormed more ideas with dog training in mind.

They fell silent as Bridges walked back into the cabin. He sat down at the table and finished the last few bites of his meal. Then he shifted and patted his stomach. "That was really good."

"Thank you." She smiled. Which boy would break first?

Both boys were trying so hard to be polite. Cooper cleared his throat. "So, when you said you needed to make a call, it seemed you were doing it to find us hay bales. Was it?"

"Nope." He gave an exaggerated yawn. "A nap sounds good about now."

"Tío Bridges!" Sebastian couldn't hold it in any longer.

Bridges laughed. "My sisters are on the July Summerfest committee."

"What's that?" The question came in stereo from either side of them.

Lilianna put her hands together. "It's been so long

since I've been. It's a huge festival for the Fourth of July. It's the first weekend of July. It takes over the town and the beach. There's music, games and tons of booths. A sand sculpture contest that is amazing. There's a rodeo and so much more. It lasts for three days." She eyed him. "What does your sister being on the committee have to do with hay bales?"

"Panaderia de Dulces usually sponsors some of the kid activities. They usually have some sort of maze or obstacle course."

The boys gasped. "At the festival?"

"Yep." He couldn't be prouder of himself.

She foresaw lots of problems. "That's only a few weeks away. They spend eight to nine months planning. You can't just pop a new activity in at the last minute."

"They already had a maze planned. The supplies have been lined up and the space mapped out. They have a company that comes in and puts it together to make sure it's safe. All this is doing is changing the layout. We have an appointment on Thursday morning for the boys to show them their work. Are y'all ready to present your designs for public use?"

The excitement rattled the roof. They were both standing and high-fiving each other. Sebastian threw his arms around Bridges. "This is awesome."

Cooper hung back, but his smile stretched his face. "We need to redraw them on that grid paper so we have the right ratios."

"Will you be ready to talk to them and show them your ideas by Thursday morning?"

Cooper nodded. "Yes. Where are we meeting them? Who are we meeting and what should I wear?" He looked down at his T-shirt and basketball shorts.

"Nothing too fancy." Bridges frowned. "We do need to get you clothes for church tomorrow."

"He's fine," Lilianna reassured them. "It's summer. If my memory is correct, we get lots of summer visitors in beachwear."

"And that's fine for them. Have you met my mother? If I take him to church dressed for a basketball game, she'll rip my ears off."

Cooper stepped back. "I don't want to upset Ms. Espinoza and I don't want to go to church."

"I don't want to go to church either. I don't know anyone." Sebastian crossed his arms and mirrored Cooper. "Can we stay here and work on our drawings?"

"No. Church is about worshipping God and fellowshipping. It helps lift up our faith." The last thing she wanted was for him to see church as a power struggle or a place he didn't belong. "All your Espinoza family will be there."

Bridges clapped his hand on Cooper's shoulder. "How about we head into town? Once we get the shopping done, we can spend a little time at the beach."

She nodded. "Afterward, you can come to our house and work on the designs with the new paper we get at the store."

Cooper nodded, then turned to Sebastian. "Let's go get your stuff from my room." The boys scurried up the ladder.

She moved to the kitchen to gather her things and wash the dishes.

"I've got this. Go relax on the front porch. We'll join you when I've got the boys ready."

"Bridges, thank you for making that call. This is such

an incredible opportunity to help them both build their confidence."

He shrugged. "Those drawings were amazing and so detailed. My sister already had the connections and the place. It's no big deal."

"It's a very big deal. But don't think this changes the fact that I know something is bothering you. Why are you shutting me out?"

He had his profile to her. She wanted to reach out and touch his jaw, to ease the tension. But she wasn't strong enough to handle the rejection when he pulled away. And she knew without a doubt that he would.

She was seeing him in a new light, and he wouldn't like it one bit. Was it his pride or a real fear of hurting her? Whatever it was, she was not giving up on him.

Bridges stared at the plate he had scrubbed five times already. She was staring at him, but he couldn't make eye contact. If he did, he'd give in and tell her everything, without being prepared.

First, he had to find out a way to know for sure that Cooper was Eduardo's son. Then they needed to be somewhere away from the boys. That would give her a chance to vent, cry, scream—or whatever—without fear of hurting them.

He knew she'd never blame Cooper. When the dust settled, he suspected she'd want to take him in and raise him as her own, right alongside Sebastian. But first, she'd have to deal with the knowledge that Eduardo had betrayed her.

His fist squeezed all the water out of the washrag. If he was experiencing this level of anger, he couldn't imagine what she was going to go through.

"Tomorrow after church, you want to go riding? We can go on the beach." He looked out the window.

"The boys would love that."

"No. I thought my mom could keep them, and it could be an adult-only thing."

"Are you asking me on a date?" She sounded horrified. But he might just be too sensitive.

He couldn't look at her. "No!" That came out harsher than he intended. "We're friends. Family. It's not a date, just a little break from 24/7 kid duty. When was the last time you did something just for you? Not work related or with Sebastian?"

She blinked at him a couple of times. "I..." She tucked her head. "I don't remember. Eduardo arranged a surprise weekend on the Riverwalk in San Antonio. Just him and me. That was years ago." She moved away and sat on a chair. She seemed stunned.

"You have friends, right? Any girls' nights out to the movies or socials at the church?" She couldn't have been that isolated. But how would he know? He'd been at a safe distance in Oklahoma.

She shook her head. "I can't think of anything. This will be my first adult-only fun since Eduardo. Maybe I need to get out more. I've been invited to several church activities, but when I had time off from work, I just wanted to be home with Sebastian."

"That makes sense. With your dad's illness, I'm sure fun wasn't on your agenda."

"No. It hasn't even been on my radar." She rose, moved toward him and touched his jaw, gently pulling him toward her until they were staring each other in the eye. "Thank you."

His throat went dry. She was so close he could see the

variation of brown streaks in her eyes. His gaze lowered to her lips. In slow motion, she leaned in and pressed her lips to his. They were so soft and had a slight flavor of fruit, cherry.

He needed to stop, but he'd waited his whole life to have her kiss him. Maybe just a moment longer.

What was he doing? With a growl, he stepped away. It was the most painful move of his life.

"Bridges?" She sounded lost and confused.

He couldn't breathe. "I've got to check on something. I'll be right back."

She followed him to the back door. "Bridges. We need to talk."

At the bottom of the step, he turned. There was enough distance to be safe. "There's nothing to talk about. You're Eduardo's wife."

Her hand went to her lips. Her eyes were wide.

Great. He felt like a complete toad. It was bad enough that he was giving her her first day out in over three years and that he was going to tear her up emotionally. But now he'd kissed her. There was no telling what she thought of him after that move.

He'd find a way to make it up to her. After he told her that he suspected that Eduardo was Cooper's father. She was really going to hate him.

Chapter Ten

The sun kissed the line between the sky and sea. Orange, yellows and pinks splashed across the clouds and reflected over the water. Bridges hadn't realized how much he missed the water and coastal air until he was sitting there with Lilianna and the boys.

Their boys. That was a traitorous thought. He rolled his neck. They were Eduardo's kids. Not his. He was just the stand-in to make sure everyone was good and safe. Never his.

And he didn't dare think about the kiss. He tried to read her mood to see if she was upset with him, but she was acting as if it had never happened.

Last Sunday had been a disaster. Sebastian had fallen ill Sunday morning, and Lilianna had kept him home. For five days, Bridges had carried the knowledge that Cooper was most likely Eduardo's. Each day it became more obvious. He kept waiting for her to see it, but she hadn't yet. Like him, she'd never in a million years think that Eduardo could have been unfaithful.

Cooper hadn't been happy about going to church without Sebastian, but Angie, Bridges's niece, had made sure he wasn't alone. And the youth pastor, Jimmy Rodrigues, went out of his way to include Cooper and make him feel welcome.

People had given Bridges questioning glances, but no one had actually asked him about Cooper's parentage. With the kid blending in with the Espinoza family so effortlessly, everyone probably assumed they knew what was going on.

His mother was the world's best at squashing any gossip anyway. She and his sister were well-known for never talking about someone out of turn. So, they enjoyed an unspoken loyalty from the entire community. It definitely came in handy when a twelve-year-old boy showed up out of nowhere and moved in with him.

Yesterday a social worker had come out to the cabin to follow up on the paperwork and do a housing inspection.

He decided to tell her what he knew about Cooper. They spent most of the time talking about the options and best course of action to keep Cooper with them.

He hadn't realized the stress he was denying. Breathing was easier. It had gone well, and he was one step closer to making sure Cooper would be safe.

Lilianna was next on his list. That was not a conversation he wanted to have.

All the things that could go wrong and all the people in his life that he couldn't protect were burning a hole in his gut.

Now it was Thursday and they sat at his sister's *panadería*, which was snuggled in the middle of connected storefronts built over a hundred years ago. A wide boardwalk separated them from the beach.

Marguerite joined them, followed by a woman who

looked all business. *"Hola."* His sister turned to Lilianna. "You remember Selena De La Rosa, right? She's married to Xavier, the oldest De La Rosa. She also happens to be mayor of our little seaside town and chair of the July Summerfest."

Shaking her hand, Lilianna smiled. "Of course. It's been a long time. I hear you also have three-year-old triplets," Lilianna said. "I feel like a total slacker."

"Oh, don't. When they say it takes a village, they mean it. And I thank God every morning and night for the wonderful people in my life who help make it all happen." She turned to the boys. "I hear you might have custom designed a maze that we get to use at the festival."

"We have six different ideas," Sebastian said proudly. Cooper sat back a little.

Selena's phone buzzed. Glancing at the text, she frowned a little. "It's a text from Irene Hernandez. She's running late. It'll take her another thirty to forty-five minutes. She's the contractor in charge of all the structures, including the maze. It's important that she sees the drawings and knows which one would work for our space. Sorry."

"That's a long time," Sebastian said, laying his head down on his crossed arms.

"Can we go to the beach while we wait? I can watch him," Cooper offered.

Lilianna put her hand on his shoulder. "How about I walk with y'all to the pier to look at the boats?" She pushed Sebastian's hair back. "You're just getting better, so we can't overdo it."

Sebastian groaned. "Mom. I feel better."

Cooper stood. "That will be cool, Bastian. Thank you for taking us."

As soon as Lilianna had the boys out of earshot, Marguerite pursed her lips and nodded. "Those two should be a couple. Am I right, Selena?" His sister pointed to him and Lilianna.

"Other than family, I try to mind my own business when it comes to personal choices." She smiled. "But y'all do fit together well."

"They would be so good together, and it would be wonderful for the boys. They need a mother and father."

"Sebastian has a father," he grumbled. Was it too late to join them on the pier?

She reached over and squeezed his arm. "Of course, he does. But I think Eduardo would fully support the idea of you and Lilianna. And I happen to know Lilianna wanted a big family. She never wanted just one child. You could give her that too."

Moving out of her reach, he dropped his head in his hands. "Will you please stop?"

Selena pushed Marguerite's coffee over to her. "Here, drink this before it gets cold. I know you love your brother and want the best for him, but I don't think he wants to talk about this."

He raised his eyes to look at Selena. "Thank you."

With a deep sigh, his sister lifted the delicate cup to her mouth, then carefully set it down. "What about the interview with the CPS caseworker? Can I ask about that?"

He sat back and scanned the boardwalk for Lilianna and the boys. "It went well. Lilianna was there, and Sharon liked the house and the setup. His case doesn't go to court for a while, and with his mother gone and him placed in a safe environment, it's not a priority. I told her I wanted to adopt him and have full custody."

"Can't you just say he's yours? Or do you think the real father would want custody if he knew? After twelve years, and with his mother passed now, will anyone ever be able to figure out who he might be?"

Bridges sat back in his chair. His sister might drive him crazy, but he also knew that she cared about him. When he'd really needed good advice, she'd always been there. He could trust her. "It's much more complicated than that." He looked at Selena. "Maybe we can talk later."

Her sister waved toward the other woman. "If you're worried about Selena, she won't talk. And she has dealt with some out-of-this-world stuff. She has great insight when it comes to human nature."

Before he could say anything, Selena stood up. "I need to make some phone calls. I'll go to the front and watch for Irene."

Marguerite turned to him. Leaning forward, she took his hand and forced his fingers to unclench. "Spill. What has you so uptight? More than normal anyway." She slapped at his arm. "I know I make you nuts, but I'm here for you. You know that, right?"

"I know for certain that Cooper is not my son. But last Saturday I realized who he belonged to." He looked across the boardwalk and scanned the area for Lilianna. The boys were ahead of her, standing next to a fisherman. They looked so similar as they stared at the water below.

Marguerite flopped back in her chair and rolled her eyes. "Seriously, you're gonna leave me with that?"

Birds flew overhead, not a care in the world. He

looked from Lilianna to his sister. "Everyone keeps commenting on how he looks like an Espinoza. He is one of us, through our cousin. I'm pretty sure he's Eduardo's son."

With a couple of blinks, she shook her head. "Eduardo's?" Her gaze went to Lillianna, Sebastian and Cooper. "How did we miss that? Now that you say it, it's so...so..."

"Obvious?"

"Yeah." Her eyes darted around, seeking an answer that he knew she'd arrive at eventually, so he didn't say anything. He sat and waited.

"So, you haven't told her yet. You could just claim him as yours, and then we'd be reassured that he was safe and being raised by family. She'll never have to know."

"Believe me, that is so tempting. No matter how I do this, she's gonna get hurt." He studied the horizon. He wanted to be somewhere with no thoughts, no problems—but that wouldn't make them go away. Or hurt the people he loved any less.

"If Jesse had a kid from when you were dating, and that kid needed a home, would you want to know?"

His sister had been happily married for thirteen years now. He couldn't imagine Jesse ever looking at another woman, but he would have said the same about Eduardo last month. He waited as she gave it careful thought.

"After I ranted and raved and maybe even threw a couple of things, I'd take the child in. It's not the kids' fault. Everyone deserves to belong in a real home. Cooper needs us. He needs his brother. They get along so well."

"Yeah. Okay, so..." He ran his fingers through his

hair and resisted the urge to pull it out. "I was going to tell her last Sunday, but Sebastian got sick. Would you and mom keep the boys after dinner? I'm gonna take her horseback riding down to the beach. When we're in the middle of the ranch, I'll tell her."

"See? You don't even need my advice. Consider it done. The boys will already be with us Sunday. How much time do you think she's gonna need?"

With a shrug, he shook his head. "She's resilient but having all night to process might be good. Can Sebastian spend the night at your place? She is going to need time. If he is already with you it'll make it easier. And it'll give her some space to cry and yell. Whatever she needs to do."

"Consider it done."

This time he took his sister's hand and squeezed. "I've been known to complain about my older sisters being bossy, but I know you've got my back. Thank you."

Over her shoulder he saw Selena, the city's mayor, waving at them. A dark-haired woman with a tight ponytail was walking beside her. "I think Irene's here."

He pulled up Cooper's backpack and handed Marguerite the notebook as the two other women joined them. "Thank you so much for talking to the boys. You don't realize the opportunity you are giving two kids who really need this right now."

Selena De La Rosa smiled. "It goes both ways. I love that two local boys are designing the maze. It is perfect for the vision I have for this festival. Engaging families and empowering children so that their dreams can come true. I'm so thankful you trusted us with their ideas."

"Go ahead and have a look. I'll go get the boys, and you can ask them questions about their work."

Halfway across the pier, he stopped. Lilianna was laughing as a gust of wind played havoc with her hair. Her light wraparound skirt danced about her. The boys were standing on the far end of the pier. Waves were hitting the rocks, and the spray was getting all three wet. They were a mess. A very happy mess.

Cooper needed them. It would devastate him if Lilianna couldn't get over Eduardo's betrayal. Maybe it would be easier if he just told everyone that Cooper was his. Then there wouldn't be any threat to the boy's relationship with Lilianna and Sebastian.

Who was he kidding? He was just protecting himself from witnessing Lilianna's pain—and from her blaming him. Avoiding the conflict wasn't going to change the truth.

Before they had left for basic training, she had asked him to watch over Eduardo and make sure that he didn't get in trouble. Why did everyone ask him to take care of the people in their lives? His father, Lilianna and Eduardo had expected too much from him.

Lilianna jumped back and laughed as the water splashed against the rocks. He didn't want to be the watchdog. He wanted to be standing with them, not as a friend looking after them but as...what? Her husband? Their dad?

Those weren't real options. Lilianna wasn't his to keep. His job was to make sure that they were safe and happy. That was all. Anything more would be dishonorable to the promise he had made Eduardo.

Eduardo was dead. It wouldn't be right to take advantage of that fact, to step into his family and steal his place—no matter how much his heart yearned for him to be the man they turned to for love and comfort.

Chapter Eleven

Lilianna took another bite of the best *fideo* in the world. No matter how hard she tried, hers was never as good as Bridges's mom's. No matter how many times she made it. The house was full of family. All of Bridges's siblings, except one, were over for Sunday's meal. There were a few extras too. Yolanda always had room for more.

Lilianna sat at the large table on the back patio. Reno had joined her, along with all the kids.

"Mom—" Sebastian sat next to her "—this is almost as good as yours!" He shoveled more into his mouth. She had to laugh.

Savannah came through the screen door and offered everyone warm tortillas. "Your mom's will always be the best, because it she adds that extra love just for you."

Lilianna smiled. Maybe it was the memories and love that made it better. Cooper took the seconds that Savannah offered him. He hadn't paused his eating since they sat down. "My mom wasn't much of a cook, but she did make the best mac and cheese. What is this? It's really good."

"*Fideo,*" Sebastian said between bites.

"Fee-day-o? I've never even seen it before."

"Really?" Sebastian's eyes were wide.

"It's my favorite meal that Abuelita makes," Angie said. "It's her mother's recipe from Mexico." She leaned forward and tried to whisper. "If they offer you *menudo*, don't take it." She wrinkled her nose and stuck out her tongue.

Reno scoffed. "Don't listen to her. It's the most divine thing you will ever eat. It cures every sort of ailment." He lifted his bowl toward Cooper.

"What's in it?"

"The most amazing flavors."

"Tripe," Angie said in disgust. "Do you know what tripe is?"

Cooper and Sebastian both shook their heads.

"It's delicious." Reno cut in and inhaled deeply through his nose. "So good. That's what it is. You scoop it up with a corn tortilla. Make sure to get the hominy and meat."

Angie crossed her arms. "It's the stomach of a cow. Gross."

Instead of being put off, Cooper looked more excited. "Cool. Does Bridges like *menudo*?"

"Of course," Reno said as he looked to Lilianna. "Where is my big brother anyway? He's usually your shadow."

"I'm not sure." He seemed to be avoiding her. "Do you both want a bowl?"

With an enthusiastic yes from the boys, she went inside. Bridges was at the stove flipping tortillas.

"Hey, stranger. The boys want to try the *menudo*. Join us?"

He kept his focus on the cast-iron griddle as he took

the last tortilla off and added it into the warmer with the others. "Sure." Moving to the left, he grabbed a couple of bowls and filled them with the soup. "Do they want lime?"

"Why not? Is that how you eat it?"

He nodded. Grabbing a couple of spoons, he headed out the door. She followed with the tortillas.

The boys sat alone. "Where did everyone go?" she asked.

"Tío Reno had a phone call, and Angie took everyone next door to her mom's house to see a movie."

"Your mother and I are about to leave. You're both staying here, so once you finish these, you can head over to watch the movie."

"Where are you going? Can we go?"

"Nope. Adults only."

Cooper smirked. "Like a date."

"No," they yelled at the same time.

Cooper grinned. "Right. Angie invited us, but we told her we wanted to wait for the *menudo*. We could take it over there so you can leave for your not-a-date date."

Bridges placed the bowls in front of the boys. "Behave. We're not in a rush. Here you go. Eat up. It'll put hair on your chest."

"Really? That's probably why Angie doesn't like it." Cooper eagerly ate up the flavorful soup with the fresh tortillas.

Sebastian still eyed him skeptically, then looked at the soup. "Do you have hair on your chest?"

Cooper grinned. "He has a bull on his chest. My mother told me."

The boys kept chatting and eating as if the world hadn't just tilted. He turned to Lilianna. Maybe she hadn't been paying attention. She fell into the chair behind her as if the bones in her legs had just melted.

No. No. No. No. No. She had heard Cooper's comment.

"What movie is the gang watching?" His heart accelerated as his gaze darted between Lilianna and the boys. She knew what that tattoo meant. He stood and held his hand out to her. "Let's go."

"I have something my mom always wore that matches your tattoo." Shyly, Cooper pulled a chain from under his shirt. "Did you give this to her?"

Lilianna gasped and covered the charm bracelet she never took off. The silver bull had been a gift from Eduardo on their graduation day. Sebastian looked confused but was hopefully too young to fully understand what this meant. "My mom has one like that."

Cooper smiled and looked at Bridges. "Is it a family thing?"

"Yep." He took Lilianna's hand and gently pulled her up. "Go ahead and head next door. I'll take your dishes in."

Breathing in short, shallow bursts, she watched the boys run off. Her eyes were large and suspiciously glossy. He squeezed her hand. "Lilianna."

Jerking her arm away, she went to the other side of the table and began stacking up more dishes. "Don't. Say. A. Word." She attacked the table with a disinfectant wipe. Arranging the chairs, he watched helplessly as she put everything in its place.

"Will you take those in?" She held out a stack of dishes. "I'll meet you at your truck." She finally looked at him briefly, then at the garden. "Are we still going horseback riding?"

"Yeah." He wanted to say so much more, but not here and not now. She was barely holding it together.

Hurrying into the kitchen, he tossed the dishes in the sink as his sister glared at him. "Hey! I just finished. You can wash those."

Grabbing her by the shoulders, he kissed the top of her head. "You know I would, but Lilianna is in the truck, waiting for me. She needs to leave now."

With a nod of understanding, she shooed him off.

Going through the house, he had to say goodbye to each person. If he missed anyone, he'd never hear the end of how rude he had grown. He was breathing hard himself by the time he opened his truck door.

Lilianna sat facing forward, her hands tightly clenched in her lap.

"Lilianna. I—"

"Don't talk. Just drive, please."

He wanted to say so much, but none of it meant anything. He backed out of his mother's driveway and went straight to the ranch. The silence was oppressive.

The guilt tore at him. Somehow, he had to make this better.

Parking in front of the barn, he tried to reach her door before she got out, but she was already outside.

Her left hand was pressed against the hardwood side of the barn, and she leaned over as though she was going to be sick.

"Lilianna." He gently took her arm to hold her up, but she jerked it away.

"Don't." She fell to her knees, her fingers tangled in her hair. The cry of a wounded animal erupted from her lungs.

His throat burned. How did he take this pain away from her? He was useless.

The cries became whimpers, and he dropped down by her side. "Lilianna. What do you want? Is there anything I can do?"

She stood and ran the back of her arm across her face. "You brought me to ride. May we do that?"

Not sure how to take this calm request after the breakdown he had just witnessed, he nodded. "Do you want to come into the barn with me?" He was reluctant to leave her alone.

She nodded and followed him.

He had a bad feeling that the worst was yet to come.

Lilianna watched Bridges move around the barn as he saddled two of the horses. He went back into the tack room and came out with two bottles of water. "We don't want to dehydrate." He winked, then took a long drink. His Adam's apple moved with each swallow.

She should have offered to help, but she didn't want to move. "It's been so long since I've been on a horse. It was with Eduardo." The words hurt coming out of her throat. Her eyes burned. But she couldn't give in to the urge to curl up on the floor and wail.

He led the two geldings to a mounting area. After he helped her up and slipped her water into a small pack tied to the saddle, he patted her leg reassuringly. "It's going to be okay."

Not wanting him to see her doubt and fear, she lifted her chin.

He left her side and swung into the saddle of a big bay. He winced. It was slight, but she saw it. "How's your shoulder?"

"Good enough." Bridges led her out of the barn area and along a trail surrounded with tall coastal grass.

She focused on the horse, the land, the sky and the man riding slightly ahead of her. His cotton shirt stretched across his shoulders, emphasizing his natural strength.

Everyone commented on how strong she was, but right now she hated that word. Just once she wanted someone else to carry the burden. She was tired of taking care of herself and everyone around her.

Eduardo had promised to always be there. He had lied. He had lied about so many things. He should be here so she could yell at him. But, as usual, it was Bridges cleaning up his mess. It was always Bridges.

Cows grazed in the distance, a huge red bull watching them. She blinked back the rush of tears. No. She turned her focus to Bridges. He didn't wear cowboy hats every day, but today he wore a gray one. Eduardo's favorite hat had been gray. It hung on a hook by her front door in San Antonio as if he were coming back. As soon as she returned there, she'd get rid of it.

Her fingers tightened around the reins, and the dun tossed his head in protest. "Sorry, boy." She relaxed and patted his neck.

Bridges turned in his saddle. "Did you say something?"

"Nope."

The concern in his eyes burned her. How long had he known? Heat rushed from her core again. No. She would not give in to the blinding anger. If she let it go, it would burn her. With a deep breath, she tried to relax.

Bridges glanced away from her and scanned the area. "There's something so connected between God and the earth when you're on the back of a horse." He sat easy in the saddle, his body moving naturally with the horse's as they slowly walked along.

She could hear the ocean but couldn't see it yet. Clouds of white spotted the blue sky. Her mouth refused to put words to all her chaotic thoughts. Bull tattoos. A charm that matched the one on her bracelet. A boy's expressive face that looked just like her son's. With more force, she swallowed down the flames that tried to flare.

"When are you going back to Oklahoma?" She bit the corner of her lip. That was not something she wanted to think about either. Something had shifted between them over the last few weeks. She wasn't too sure yet what it was or what it meant, but she knew there was something different.

They had kissed, and it had meant something. His ignoring it didn't change that fact.

Not that it mattered. He would be leaving her, just like everyone else. "Thank you for not giving me any platitudes. People like to tell me that God doesn't give me more than I can handle. I loathe everything about that saying."

He pulled up so they were side by side. "We weren't meant to do it alone. As humans, we're frail. We all are. I've thought all day about what Pastor Rod said today. 'You're not alone. I'm here with you.'" Bridges paraphrased. "It's so simple but powerful."

"It's Hebrews 13:5. I need to post that one on my mirror. There are so many days filled with loneliness." With a harsh laugh, she shook her head. "You're an island of one man. It doesn't seem as if anyone is allowed on your beaches for too long."

He stiffened.

She didn't want to argue. Not with him. "I'm sorry. I know better than anyone how difficult it can be to let others in. How much longer are you in Port Del Mar?"

"Not sure. Are you ready to talk about it?" He tilted his head to look at the sky, then he turned to her. "Eduardo and Cooper."

"No." Her stomach knotted, and her stupid eyes burned.

One of the things she knew about Bridges was that he would do anything to keep his family and the people he cared for happy. "Why didn't you tell me?"

She waited for words that would explain what she would have said was impossible. She straightened her spine and looked at the waves. One rolled into another, then they went back out to sea. "He's twelve, Bridges."

The stubborn man still didn't say anything. Birds flew over as the breeze cooled her hot skin. "Have you always known?"

"No. I had planned to tell you today. That's why I asked Marguerite to keep the boys."

A cry escaped. She covered her mouth. "Your family knows? I don't understand." She laughed. "I finally get my little lifeboat righted, and then, in one minute, it's upside down again. How long have you realized it? Is that why you went as soon as they called? Did you know?" She choked, unable to say it.

"I had no clue." Bridges adjusted his hat and stood in the saddle. "Damian is actually the one that noticed. He doubted my story that Cooper couldn't be mine. He said the kid moved too much like me not to be related." He took a deep breath. "Once he pointed it out, I don't know how we missed it, other than we didn't want to see it. Today was the first time he mentioned the tattoo or the silver charm." Their horses stopped. "Lilianna, Cooper is Eduardo's son."

"There has to be another explanation."

He just sat there, wanting to hold her and tell her it was all going to work out, but he couldn't stomach any more lies. "'Trust in the Lord with all thine heart; lean not onto thine own understanding. In all thy ways acknowledge him and he shall direct thy paths.'"

"Are you quoting the Bible to me?"

"It's one my mom always said. She made us memorize it. My words are useless. I thought you'd be better off hearing the words of God. I'm never sure of the verse."

"I think it's in Proverbs. I'll have to look it up and tattoo it on my wrist where I can always see it. Because I don't understand any of this."

"I don't either. I'm struggling with the whole idea."

She nodded. "He cheated on me. I've been that woman who bragged about the faithfulness of my husband. He had his faults, but I never imagined he would be turn to another woman."

"This happened before you were married. He was eighteen. It's not an excuse, but he did grow up. He adored you."

"Our marriage started out on a lie." She heard her voice get louder and higher, but she couldn't stop. "How can I trust anything he told me?"

"Lilianna. He loved you. I—"

"Stop. Don't say another word about him. There is an anger so deep right now I don't know if I can contain it. If I let it go, the ugliness inside me will lash out at you. I just want to go home and cry."

Her hands were tight on the leather reins. Taking a

deep breath, she relaxed her body. "I. Hate. Crying. I hate Eduardo for being dead. I hate you for…" A sob rent the air. Her horse sidestepped from the unconscious pressure she was applying to his sides.

Bridges was off his horse and at her side. He took the poor animal's reins. "Come here. You can hate me as much as you need to. I can take it." He reached for her.

Shaking, she swung her leg over the saddle and fell against him. She pressed her fist against his chest. Then she saw the charm. The silver bull.

She pulled at it, trying to rip it off. "He said that he'd always be mine. He was my *toro*. But he gave her one of these too, and a baby. Did he give her his heart? Why? How many did he give to other women?" Her throat hurt from the sobbing and yelling.

Bridges took her hand and gently removed the leather charm bracelet. He slipped it into his front pocket, then pressed his lips to the spot on her wrist where she had scratched herself.

Her breaths were shallow and hard to catch. Sobs filled the air. Her sobs. She had lost control of everything, even herself. In her anger, she hit her fist against Bridges chest. "Why are you just standing there?"

She knew her anger at Bridges was irrational, but there wasn't anyone else to take it out on. Eduardo was out of her reach. Her sobs became hiccups as she collapsed against the safe wall of her best friend.

As she quieted, the sounds around her came into focus. The waves and katydids made a promise that everything would keep moving forward, even if she wanted the world to stop and just let her grieve another loss.

He cupped the back of her head and held her close.

"I'm mad at him too. I'm angry that he's not here to make it right. It's another mess he left for us to clean up."

The world was dark; just the thundering of Bridges's heart kept her grounded. "Can we stay here forever?"

His hands caressed her hair. "That would be nice, but we have two boys who need us."

She pushed away from him. "The boys. Cooper still believes he's yours."

"He will be mine. But he's Eduardo's too."

She looked away with a faint nod. "Take me home. I have to think what this all means. I need—" She needed Eduardo to explain this to her. Her horse was grazing nearby. Without help this time, she mounted.

They were high above the beach. "Is there a way to the beach?"

He nodded and swung his horse north. "This way."

"How much longer will it take? I need to go pick up Sebastian."

"No, you don't. Marguerite is keeping him for a sleepover. You have the whole night to yourself. When was the last time you only had you to worry about? Take a long bath, sleep in, do whatever you want."

"What do they think? Marguerite and your mom?"

Bridges rubbed his face and then urged the horses forward. "They know you're strong, and that no matter what, you'll be fine. We'll get the boys through this."

Strong. The word made her want to hurl her lunch. But there wasn't anything else to do. He was right about one thing. She'd get through it and so would Sebastian. And Cooper.

All three of them had had life lessons in survival.

Chapter Twelve

They sat in silence on the ride back to his mother's house. Her brain couldn't put any verbal thoughts together. No words. Crying wiped a person out. After Eduardo's death, it had been Sebastian and work that got her out of bed on the days she wanted to stay under her covers.

"Thank you for making sure Sebastian was taken care of tonight." She did need the extra time to get her head back in the game.

He turned, then slowed as he approached her place. "You want me to drop you off?"

"No. I want to say good-night to Sebastian. I need to hug him, but I can walk from there."

"No. It's getting dark. I'll pick up Cooper and take you." The cars that had filled his mother's driveway and surrounded the house earlier were gone. "Will it be too hard to be in the truck with Cooper? I wasn't thinking. I'm sorry."

"No. It's fine. This is not his fault. I'm glad he found us."

He reached across and took her hand. "You know

what they say about self-care, right? You can't tend anyone else if you're worn out. There aren't any words to
make it right, but I'm so sorry about all of this."

"Stop apologizing. It's not your responsibility. I just
want to go home." At Marguerite's, she followed the
children's laughter to the back of the house. Bridges's
sister hugged her, and Lilianna was grateful that she
didn't say anything. She found Sebastian in Josh's room.
She froze outside the doorway.

Cooper was on the top bunk, bombing their fort of
sheets with rolled-up socks. He moved and sounded like
Eduardo.

She couldn't step into the room. How had she missed
it?

"Mom! I thought I was spending the night. Please?"
Sebastian sounded devastated. He had become so withdrawn in San Antonio. Her hope had been that the Espinozas would work their family magic, just like they
had done all those years ago for a girl so sad she didn't
think she would ever be happy again.

"I just stopped by to say good night."

"Oh." He scrambled from the fort and hugged her.
"Good night." Then, just as quick, he was crawling back
through the flap.

"I'll come get you for lunch."

"Okay," he yelled from within the structure.

"He can stay all day." Marguerite patted her arm.

"Yeah, Mom. Let me stay. We have plans."

"We'll see."

Bridges came up behind her. He had been talking to
his brother-in-law. "Come on, Coop. Time to go."

"Why can't I stay?" He frowned from the top bunk.

"We've got an early morning schedule for the animals tomorrow. You said you wanted to help. You can overnight another time."

He climbed down and followed Bridges to his truck. Once inside, with everything in her, she had to fight the urge to cry while Cooper chatted about his day and the animals.

The world outside her window moved in slow motion. She wasn't ready for this. Bridges kept giving her nervous glances. As soon as he stopped, she was out of the small space and across her yard. Bridges stayed until he saw her lights come on in the house.

She stood at the front window and watched them drive away. Then she slid to the floor and cried.

After a long bout of tears, she lit candles and soaked in the tub. But questions crowded her brain. Sitting on the back porch, she read from her devotional, but she couldn't stay focused. Unable to escape her thoughts, she got in the car and drove along the shoreline. Close to midnight, she stood in front of Bridges's cabin. The one he shared with her husband's son.

The anger was being replaced with confusion and he had answers. Should she knock? Call? What if she woke Cooper?

She walked to the side of the cabin and tapped on Bridges's bedroom window. Nothing. She tried again. There was no way he was this sound of a sleeper. What about Big Mack? Wouldn't he bark to let them know someone was outside the cabin?

"Lilianna?"

She jumped, her hand on her chest. "Bridges, you scared me."

"Well, I thought I had some sort of intruder. What are you doing out here?"

"I had a complete meltdown. Then I started thinking. I can't stop it. I have so many questions, and you're the closest I'll ever get to answers."

With a sigh, he took her hand and led her to the back porch. "Cooper's less likely to hear us back here."

"Where's Big Mack?"

"He sleeps with Coop. When I first heard noises, I checked to make sure Cooper wasn't sneaking out. I told Mack to stay with him."

She curled her legs under her as she settled onto the big rocker, the pillow in her lap.

He reached for her hand.

"Don't." She jerked away from his touch. Anger burst through her. "You're in the picture with her. You knew her." Her throat was raw. She was so afraid of the truth, but the need to know was eating her up inside. "This was a mistake." Pulling her feet out, she went to stand, but Bridges calmly laid a hand on her leg.

"No. You have questions. Ask me anything. We can work through this together. If you leave, you'll just be in your own head and I'll worry about you driving."

With a sigh, she did stand, but she moved to the edge of the porch and leaned against the railing. Darkness surrounded the cabin. Above, stars were scattered across the sky like silver glitter. "The darker it is, the more the stars shine. With all the security lights in the city, the starlight is washed out and faded."

He joined her, relaxing next to her but still giving her space. "It reminds me that we're just a minuscule part of a big universe and of God's promise to always be there for us. Even in the midst of our darkest moments."

Unable to indulge the yearning to lean into him, she went back to the rocking chair. She folded her hands between her knees to keep them from reaching for his warmth. "Bridges, I need complete honesty from you, no matter how much the truth hurts. I have to get past this. Promise me."

"I'll tell you everything I know." The gentle heat of his hand settled on her shoulder. She reclined back in the rocker, breaking the contact. If she let him touch her now, she would fall apart in his arms again.

"Did you know about Cooper's mother? What was she like?" What had Eduardo seen in the other woman that she didn't have? That was the real question, but she didn't want to sound too pathetic. She forced a harsh laugh. "Of course, you knew her. You're in the picture."

"I don't really remember much about her. I've been running that time over and over in my head. Trying to pull up memories that weren't important enough to store properly. She was just one of the girls that hung out where the soldiers would go for a little R and R." He sat on the porch step and settled against the railing with his arm draped over his bent knee. "She had an outrageous laugh and was super friendly."

She scoffed. "I'm sure. She was more fun than me?"

"Don't do that. It had nothing to do with you. Eduardo was impulsive, immature and made bad choices when we were younger. Looking back, I don't think it lasted long. About a month before we left. Eduardo was avoiding me too. He was going into town without me." He squinted. "I might have met her once or twice. She probably confused our names and Eduardo didn't correct her."

He tilted his head. "Remember when you called me

because you were worried about Eduardo being distant? It was about a month before we left Georgia."

Her jaw was hurting. She tried to relax. No success. "I do. You told me not to worry, that Eduardo loved me and was just feeling stressed." She wanted to blame someone. That would make it easier. "You were there. How could you not know?" She knew it was irrational, but she felt just as betrayed by Bridges.

He shrugged and looked over his shoulder. "Believe me, that question is on a repeat loop in my head. Was there something I missed? He was avoiding both of us. Obviously, he was ashamed of what he was doing." He stood up, turned his back to her and braced his hands on the railing. He dropped his head. "He let her believe he was me." A disgusted sound tore from his chest. "He'd done some harebrained stunts, but…" He shook his head. "I wouldn't have thought he'd do this."

"How long have you known Cooper was his?"

"It was just like I told you. Since last weekend. Damian saw it. I'm as shocked by this as you are. It was right there in front of me, but my brain wouldn't allow me to even consider it."

She sniffed as if trying not to cry. "My husband cheated on me and left a child behind. What am I supposed to do about that? All my memories are tainted. Was our whole marriage and his love a lie?"

"Lilianna. Don't."

"And there's a child. He has a name. He's in my life. What do we do with Cooper now?"

A thud sounded in the cabin. Her hand flew to her mouth. "Was that—?"

Bridges was already past her and inside the kitchen. She rushed into the cabin behind him, ready to help

Cooper understand that she wasn't upset with him. He had to know that no matter what, this was his home and they were his family.

Bridges was on one knee scratching Big Mack behind the ear. "It was just the dog."

"Are you sure?"

He walked to the ladder and went far enough up to check inside the loft. Then he slowly came down and went to the porch. Mack stayed at his side. He carefully closed the door behind them. "He's still asleep. We must have heard Mack jumping down."

"I should go. No amount of talking will change what Eduardo did. He's not even here to... I don't know." Waving her hand at the useless thought floating around her head. "Explain. Apologize." Her legs collapsed under her, and she fell back onto the rocking chair. "Nothing can wash away what I know now. There's a permanent change that exposes our life as a lie. What if Eduardo never even loved me? He was always running off..." Her chest heaved again as she tried to catch her breath.

"No." Bridges fell to his knees in front of her. He cupped her face to make sure they were eye to eye. "This is one thing that happened before you were married. Eduardo was an eighteen-year-old boy far from home for the first time. It wasn't easy. He messed up. But he came back to you. He devoted the rest of his life to you." He rested his forehead against hers. "He loved you. Please don't even think otherwise." His voice was low and guttural.

He stood and brought her up with him, his arms and body surrounding her with warmth. She closed her eyes and let him hold her. Protect her from all the hurt. She wanted to beg him to never let her go, but life didn't work that way.

"What do we do now?" she whispered. "He's Eduardo's son. Sebastian's brother. We're his family. What happens when you go back to Oklahoma?" It was dangerous how dependent she was becoming on him. Life had taught her early on always to be prepared for people to leave her.

"We have time to figure it out." His large hand cupped the back of her head. He gently caressed her hair in a soothing motion. "I promised Eduardo I'd take care of his family. I'm not going to leave you alone with this."

"And Cooper?" Moving her head back, she looked up at him.

"We're keeping him." He grinned.

He'd always been in her heart, but something shifted. He was so much more than a friend, than Eduardo's cousin.

Searching his eyes, all she found was bone-deep commitment and compassion for his family. That's all he saw her as: another responsibility. She wanted him to see her.

Leaning forward, she touched his cheek. When he frowned at her, she almost backed off, but she was tired of holding herself back. Of not allowing herself to feel.

Closing her eyes, she crossed the line and pressed her lips to his. They were so tender and soft. At first, he didn't move. Remained stiff.

She wasn't going to pull away this time. Leaning in, she silently implored him to kiss her back. With a low moan, his arms moved to her waist and he delved into the moment, joining her.

She felt so right in his arms. More alive than she had in years.

* * *

He had her in his arms, was kissing her, after all these years. The love he had kept buried resurfaced. Like a lost treasure chest. But it wasn't his to open.

She was too vulnerable tonight.

Breaking contact with her lips, he rested his forehead against hers. Their hard breaths mirrored each other. Pulling back, he forced himself to look her in the eyes.

That was wrong. He forgot all the reasons he shouldn't be kissing her. Everything he'd ever wanted was shining in the depths of her gaze.

Shutting his eyes, he severed the contact. Stiffening his resolve, he stepped away with his hands fisted. They were going to get him in trouble. "Sorry. That was a mistake."

"A mistake?" Pain sharpened her words. "I'm a mistake?"

"No! That's not what I meant. Kissing you. I shouldn't have… It won't happen again. I promise." The porch was too small. He had to get to more space. Turning away from her, he went down the steps.

Her hand gently touched his arm. He held still, not wanting to cause any more hurt to a woman who had already been handed too much for one life.

"Bridges, I'm the one that kissed you. I'm sorry if I took advantage of the situation. I'm just so…" She wrapped her arms around her middle. She looked alone and isolated. Not what he wanted, but his nerves were too raw and exposed at the moment to comfort her. He was being a selfish jerk.

Eduardo had betrayed her, and now Bridges was letting them both down.

"You're Eduardo's girl. I promised him I'd look after

you and Sebastian if anything ever happened. It happened, and now he has made this even bigger mess and he's not here." Turning from her, he searched the horizon. No, she deserved him to at least look her in the eye. He faced her. "Our emotions were running high, and I crossed a line. Our focus is on Sebastian and Cooper. This other stuff between you and me is emotional confusion."

"You're probably right." She sounded so cold. "Thank you for everything you've done for us. It's fair to say that you've gone far above the call of duty. I'll let you go back to bed. There's nothing else we can do tonight. You have PT tomorrow afternoon. How about you and Cooper come a little early and we can have lunch on my back porch?"

"Are you sure you're okay to keep Cooper for me? I can ask my mom."

She turned on him, her finger pushing against his chest. "Don't you dare. Yes. He's just a boy and he needs us. We're the only family he has." Standing straighter, she shifted away from him. "The thought of what Eduardo did has gutted me, but it's not Cooper's fault. Plus, I'm strong, right?" She lifted her chin. "We will do the right thing. Like you said earlier, we already love him. This doesn't change that."

He advanced toward her. She turned and went to her car.

Holding her door as she climbed in, he wanted to comfort her. "You don't have to be strong all the time."

She gave him the saddest smile. It tore at his heart.

"Bridges, sometimes it's the only option." She started the engine and grabbed the handle, then paused and looked up at him. "You're my best friend. I can't lose you."

"I'm right here. Text me when you get home."

"I'm just going down the road."

"Text me." He stood watching until her taillights had disappeared.

Returning to the cabin, he rubbed his shoulder. It was too soon for more pain pills. He sat on the foot of his bed and tried to pray.

With her gone, there was an emptiness he couldn't fill. Mack placed a paw on his leg. "Yeah. I know. I don't think she'll ever be out of my head."

When was the last time he'd been free of this heavy weight that sat on his shoulders, the last time he'd been truly happy, without the shadow of dread? Had there ever been a time when he hadn't carried this burden of not being able to protect the people he loved?

Memories surfaced of exploring the ranch or going out on the ocean in kayaks with Eduardo and Lilianna. He had to go all the way back to the days before his father had told him he was sick. Before that day, his only concern had been which adventure Eduardo would take Lilianna and him on next.

He flopped back on the bed and stared at the ceiling. There was no way he was going to get any sleep tonight. Normally on nights like this, he'd jump in Eduardo's truck and go on a late-night ride to nowhere and talk to his best friend. But he couldn't leave Cooper. Still, if he stayed in the house, he'd end up waking him.

With a sigh as heavy as his thoughts, he went to the front porch. The big black King Ranch truck shone in the moonlight. Toro.

With Eduardo's son asleep in the cabin, there

wouldn't be any midnight trips. He went to the pickup and placed his hand on the hood. They had spent so many hours laughing and planning out their life in this truck. It was where he'd promised Eduardo that he'd watch over Lilianna and Sebastian.

Now he had Cooper, and his feelings for Eduardo's wife kept resurfacing. If Eduardo was here, they'd be inside and driving until they had talked it out.

He climbed into the driver's seat and pressed his head against the steering wheel. Maybe he could rant and yell at Eduardo like he had so many times when his friend was alive. "Eduardo, how do I stop this vicious cycle in my head? I'm so angry at you right now. Why couldn't you take the time to think about your actions? You never thought past the moment."

All the anger he'd buried for Eduardo boiled to the surface. "If I couldn't love Lilianna, why did you leave her? You had no business dying. Cheating on Lilianna." He slammed his fist against the dashboard, welcoming the pain that shot through his shoulder "How could you? You left two boys without a father and one boy without a home." His throat was raw from yelling.

Spent and exhausted, he slumped back. It would be easy to blame everything on Eduardo. Even the kiss.

Because of Eduardo's jerk move, Lilianna was using him to lash out. She was vulnerable, and returning that kiss only confused them more.

In truth, he was just as angry at himself for not being able to fix this for her.

He'd do anything for her, but he might not survive all this once she worked it out and wanted to go back to being friends. He couldn't allow the kiss to change his resolve.

Flipping down the visor, he caught the picture he kept hidden. It was tucked away, but easy to find when he needed a reminder of his promise.

The edges were worn from him holding it. It had been taken by his sister on the day Eduardo and Lilianna had gotten married. They had been dancing, and Eduardo had swung her out. Her dress and hair were swirling around her. Love and laughter radiated from her. Pure joy. That's what she deserved.

He rubbed his eyes. There would be no crying. That was a waste of time and allowed weakness to sneak in. He blinked and looked to the eastern sky. The sun would be coming up in a couple of hours.

Mack rested his head on his thigh and whined. "Yeah, we need to go check on Cooper and then try to get some sleep."

Climbing out of Eduardo's truck, he moved slowly. He felt like he was a hundred years old. Mack ran to the door. Once inside, he charged up the ladder. Even though it leaned, the dog's ability was still a feat, and Bridges smiled at the sight.

Up in the loft, Mack ran to the edge and barked with an urgency that had Bridges' heart rate doubling, "What is it, boy?" In a matter of seconds, he was calling for Cooper and climbing the rungs.

No response. The loft was empty. Not only was Cooper not in his bed but the dresser stood open. Everything was gone, along with his backpack.

Chapter Thirteen

Cooper was gone. Fear had Lilianna's hand shaking, but she couldn't move fast enough. Bridges was still talking to her when she got into her car. "Go get him. I'll be right behind you," she pleaded. "I'm not far. I know in my gut that he'll need me. And you. He'll need us both to resolve this crisis. He didn't understand what he overheard."

"He understood. What he didn't get was how we feel about him." Bridges's voice was grim. Mack barked. "It looks as if he took the trail behind the barn. Can you call my mother and the police?"

"We need to call his caseworker too. Let her know what's going on." Dread filled her. "We'll have to tell them why he ran. We hid the truth. This won't look good."

"I already told them."

"Before…" She cleared her head. That didn't matter tonight. "I'll phone everyone and be right there. Bridges, please find him."

"I will."

She hung up. How could Cooper understand any of

this? He was a child and she, an adult, didn't even understand it. What broke her heart was that he hadn't trusted them enough to stay and ask questions. He'd run. What could she have done to make this a safer place for him?

What if he was hurt or they didn't find him? She knew that, in the blink of an eye, someone could be gone from this world forever. Fear constricted her chest.

There was no time to give in to those feelings. She flew over the cattle guards and pulled up, trailing a big cloud of dust behind her. Jumping from her car, she ran to the barn, but she didn't see anyone.

Flashlight in hand she ran behind the barn. Mack's barking was loud and clear.

Running on the trail, she was grateful for her tennis shoes. Bridges came into view.

"You got here in record time." Bridges and Mack came around the corner.

She nodded trying to catch her breath. "Does Mack have a scent?"

"Yeah. Hopefully this will be quick."

"Why would he go to an isolated beach?" She followed as Mack kept his nose on the ground. "Do you think he's just taking a night walk or running away? He wouldn't leave us, would he?"

"He's running. He took everything with him. The noise we heard must have been him."

"But you checked on him and he was in his bed." Her heart was pounding in her ears. "So, he waited. I would've thought you'd be a light sleeper. Neither you nor Mack heard him leave?"

"We were sitting in the truck for a couple of hours. If I had been inside, where I was supposed to be…"

"Oh." So, he had been as upset as she had, either

about the kiss or Eduardo's lies. "You can't blame your-self."

Bridges sighed as they followed Mack. "I was hop-ing he went to your house."

"He still could. Your mother is there in case he shows up. But if he ran from you, I think he'd run from me too. It's so dark out here. Where do you think he's going?"

"I don't know. There's a good chance he has no clue."

They fell silent, and all the horrible things that could happen to a young boy out by himself in the night ran through her mind. Her eyes burned. "There are so many—"

"Don't go there." Bridges's voice was calm and solid. "We're gonna find him. Maybe he's trying to find his way back to town. Damian is going down to saddle a horse, and as soon as there's enough light, several people will be looking for him. Hopefully we'll—"

Mack's barking hit a new level, and he jumped at the end of the leash.

"Cooper?" They both shouted his name at the same time.

Lilianna lifted her flashlight. At the edge of the beam of light, Cooper turned and looked at them, his eyes wide. She ran. He didn't move, just stood there and let her wrap him in her arms. Now she was full-on crying. "Oh, Cooper. Don't ever do that again. I was so scared."

Mack was jumping on them, his tail wagging as he barked his own greeting. Cooper hugged the dog, fall-ing to his knees as Mack licked his face.

Bridges was breathing hard. "Do you know how dan-gerous it is to be out here alone at night in the dark? Why would you sneak out like that?"

Cooper was trembling. The warm breeze wasn't the

reason. He looked at her with eyes so full of sadness that it broke her heart. She cupped his face. "Don't ever do that again. Don't run from us."

Big Mack was wagging his tail and running in circles around the boy.

"Come on. Let's go back to the cabin and talk there. We need to make a few calls and clear up any misunderstandings."

"Calls. Are you sending me away?" Cooper stiffened. "I don't want to go back—"

"No. You're not going anywhere." Bridges's voice was flat, no emotion whatsoever. She'd heard him like that only a few times in their lives. It was a clear sign that his emotions were overwhelming him and he couldn't deal.

"If you didn't want to be returned to CPS, then why would you run?" Bridges stopped in the middle of the trail and turned to them. "They let you stay with me because it was safe. If I can't keep you in my house, then why would they let me keep you?"

"But it's not your fault I ran. I—"

"You are my responsibility, and I failed." His jaw was popping as he stared at them, his lips in a tight, thin line.

She could see the angst, but she was afraid that all Cooper saw was anger. "Bridges. We have him, he's safe."

"I'm not yours. I never was." A sob creaked the boy's last word. "My mom lied. She lied about everything. She was nothing but a—"

Bridges swiveled back to walk the trail and grabbed Cooper into a tight hug. "She was your mother." His big hands held Cooper close. "She was your mother, and we'll talk about this when we get home." His ribs expanded and fell back with each heavy breath. He was close to losing it, and she knew he never did that in front of people.

After a moment of listening to the wind and waves, she put one arm around Cooper and the other hand on Bridges. She made sure her voice was soft and low. "We think that Eduardo lied to your mom."

Silently, Bridges urged them to move forward. With the flashlight illuminating the path home, she started to breathe easier. They had Cooper. He was safe. "We were both so scared. Where were you trying to go?"

"I don't know. I thought I'd have more time before you noticed I was gone. But it's so dark out here, I didn't know which direction to go." His head hung low. "Why did you even bother to come look for me?"

Bridges turned back to them and cupped Cooper's face. "I promise that I'll always come for you. Day or night."

"Why? My own mother didn't even do that." Cooper pulled away from them and stepped back. His eyes were puffy and red.

Bridges followed him and gently put an arm around the boy's shoulders. "Once we get to the house and call everyone, we'll have a long talk."

"Everyone?"

"We called the police and my family."

As they passed the barn, a few of the horses called out to them. Bridges had his cell out and was phoning everyone to let them know they had Cooper. Reaching the top step of the porch, Cooper collapsed, hugging his overstuffed backpack to him.

Lilianna sat down on his left side and put an arm around him. Mack got as close as he could and laid his muzzle on his leg, looking up at him with total adoration. The boy buried his face in the dog's fur and cried, sobs shaking his shoulders.

Bridges was on the phone with his mother. "Get some sleep. Thanks for helping." He tapped a few buttons on his phone, then looked down at the boy. "Cooper, you're fine."

The boy lifted his gaze and aggressively wiped his face. Anger and bitter resolve were etched on the soft brown skin. "Why'd you call the cops? Do you want them to take me away?"

Bridges slipped his cell into his pocket and lowered himself to the bottom step. He leaned against the railing and closed his eyes. "I didn't call the police to pick you up. I needed to let them know we found you so they can stop looking."

"I'm… I'm going back to the foster home?"

"Nope. You're stuck with me. What did you hear that made you think you had to leave?"

"I heard the truth. I'm not yours." His voice caught, and he lowered his head to hide his face in Mack's fur. "The man who got my mom pregnant was a liar. He was Lilianna's husband." He turned away from her. "He lied to my mom and Lilianna. That man is my…"

She caressed the boy's hair. "He wasn't my husband when he met your mother. You know, this makes you and Sebastian real brothers."

"How can you even look at me? Sebastian thinks his father is a hero. Not a cheater and liar. It'd be best for everyone if I just disappeared."

Her arms went around him as she pulled him against her. "That's not true. You're part of our family. An important part to us all. How do you think Sebastian's going to feel if he wakes up and finds out that you disappeared from his life without a word?"

"I was a mistake. How's he going to feel when he finds out that—?"

"Stop." Bridges' stern voice had them both sitting straighter.

Bridges moved to the step below Cooper. His large hand gently lifted the boy's face until they were eye to eye. "You belonged to this family before we knew you carried our blood. And one rule we have never gets broken. We don't turn our backs on each other. People make mistakes, but they are never the mistake. You're a gift from God, just like Sebastian and everyone else in the family. God brought you to us when we needed you and you needed us."

"Why would you want me? How can I be what you need?"

"You're already my son. You were from the minute I took you from the police station. I had already made plans for you to stay with us. I'll fight for you if I have to."

Cooper didn't say anything, but the loneliness haunting his eyes tore at her.

She couldn't hold back. "I love you, Cooper."

The boy made a face like he didn't believe her. She sighed. He'd probably heard those words from his mother, so they didn't mean much.

"Don't believe her?" Bridges leaned back and looked at the sky. Was her expression so easy to read, or did he just know her that well? "Words are easy, right?"

With one arm around the dog, Cooper nodded.

"Then look at our actions. You're part of us in everything we do. Family doesn't run away. We stay and talk."

Lilianna smiled. "We might move out of town, but we always come back."

Bridges shot her a glare, then shook his head. "So, Cooper. Ask us whatever you want. Anxiety of the unknown is what lurks in the dark and keeps us from living our dream. What's your greatest fear and what's your dream?"

The sounds of the night surrounded them. No one spoke for several minutes. Lilianna was about to say something—anything—when Bridges cleared his throat.

"Revealing our fears and dreams is a powerful action, and we can only do it with people we trust completely. So, I get why you hold them close."

"I ain't afraid of anything," Cooper blurted. "Dreams are for babies that don't know better."

"Everyone has fears. The biggest cowards make themselves feel bigger by keeping you down while acting like they don't have any. I know a few men like that. What about you? Do you know any?"

Cooper shrugged and hugged Big Mack.

"How about I tell you mine?"

"You're scared? Of what? You're so strong. You even survived a bullet. Are you afraid of getting shot again?"

"That's a good question." Bridges stretched out his legs in front of him and crossed his ankles like he was settling in for a nice long conversation. There was no hint that they hadn't had any decent sleep all night.

"I haven't really let myself think about it. But that could be there, buried under other stuff. I'll need to think about it hard. One of the things that keeps me from sleeping is letting my family down."

"But you're awesome and they love you." He sounded outraged on Bridges's behalf.

Lilianna leaned deeper into the hug she had going and laid the side of her head against Cooper's. He relaxed into her. She tried to make eye contact with Bridges to let him know they were getting to him.

Her heart tripped over itself. He had always been in her life. Quiet and steady in the background.

"My dad died of cancer when I was your age. About a year before, he told me what the doctor said, but he didn't want my mom or sisters to know. He didn't want to do any treatments. He thought this would be the best way to create happy memories for them. So, he depended on me to take care of anything that came up."

The tears clogged her throat at the thought of her friend being so alone and scared with that huge responsibility. "Does she know now?" she had to ask.

"No. That's part of what frightens me. I have to protect the people I love—but sometimes, no matter how hard I try, I could fail. Cooper, you're part of my family. I can't fail, but I don't know how to protect you and keep you happy if you run away."

"I'm sorry. I didn't mean to make you afraid."

"Thank you."

"What about dreams?"

With a heavy sigh, he tilted his head back and closed his eyes. "I completely understand being afraid of having hopes. Maybe some are never meant to come true. But I have one that I thought might be out of reach, but now I think it might be happening."

"Really?"

"I've always wanted a kid of my own, but I didn't see how. You know, without a wife and everything."

Tears dripped onto Big Mack. She wasn't sure if they were hers or Cooper's. Bridges shifted and held his arms open. With a whimpering sound, Cooper slid out of her arms and into Bridges's. "I'm really yours?"

"If you let this dream come true, then you're mine and I'm yours."

"Can I call you dad?" His voice was muffled against Bridges's shirt.

"I'd like that."

Now she was truly crying. What other things had he longed for that he'd never shared?

She scooted closer and put her arms around them both.

"I have a fear," Cooper said, so quietly she barely heard him.

"The only way we can fight it is by putting it out in the open. What is it?" Bridges' voice made her believe that they could claim victory in any battle if he was by her side.

"What if CPS takes me away? Did I mess up? I'll tell them it's all my fault."

"I don't think so. But if the worst happens, if CPS takes you away, I'll come for you. You'll never be alone again. Just know that I might not be right by your side, but I'm doing everything I can to get you back."

She kissed Cooper's forehead. "We're your family now. Families look different, and when this all gets settled, I'm not sure what ours will look like exactly, but you're with us. It's okay to be afraid. We'll work through this together. I promise."

Cooper was safely at home, wrapped in Lilianna's arms as she softly reassured him of his place with them all. Bridges relaxed for the first time in twenty-four hours. Everything was going to be okay.

The only thing wrong in this moment was this burning deep in his gut. He felt as though he wanted to cry. Whether he was happy, sad or angry, he wasn't sure. Maybe all three at once.

Emotions were messy, and when they came out around Lilianna, they were dangerous. The last thing he needed was to get emotional around her.

His job was to protect his best friend's widow. He had managed to keep his feeling to himself this long; he could do it for another thirty years to keep her safe. The talk of fears and dreams had hit too close.

His longing for being a father was real, but he could only see her as the mother in his little family. His was a dream that betrayed his best friend, a man who was killed in the line of duty. He should have been with Eduardo. If he had, maybe Eduardo would have come home to his wife and Sebastian.

Lilianna cuddled against Cooper, giving him the comfort, a lost boy craved. She was such a good mother, a fierce warrior who wouldn't let the child drown in his fears, no matter how much she was hurting.

She winked at him over Cooper's head. "Enough adventure and bonding tonight. It's time for my boys to go to bed." She stood and held out her hand to Cooper. "What about a small bedtime story before I leave? It can help calm an overactive brain after all this drama."

"I'm too old for that." He looked to Bridges.

"You're never too old for a good story. I'd like to hear one."

"I can tell you a Bible story about a prodigal son."

"What does *prodigal* mean?"

"Wasteful or reckless, I think. It's about a son that leaves home and does all these things his father warned him not to do. He loses everything and has nowhere to go, so he returns."

Curled up on the sofa, she told him the sad story of two ungrateful sons, the one who had everything but whose jealousy stole his joy and the other who took what he had for granted.

Was he the bitter son who did all the right things out of duty and was jealous of Eduardo?

Listening to her voice, his own mind settled. Cooper's eyes kept closing. *"Mijo."* She gently caressed his hair. "Let's get you upstairs. I'll finish the story there."

With a nod they went up, followed by Mack. Bridges went to the front porch and waited for her.

She came down alone, and he handed her a cup of coffee.

He stared at the cream swirled into the black liquid in his cup. "Thank you for being here. You were right. He needed you."

She took a sip and closed her eyes, a total-bliss moment. "He needed you too. You're going to be an awesome father, Bridges."

He scoffed. "No. I'm pretty sure I'm going to mess it up. I don't know how not to be like my father. He was a good man, but…"

Stepping in front of him, she stopped his pacing and lifted his chin. "He was. But he was closed off emotionally. He had no business saddling a young boy with the burdens he placed on you. You need to tell your mother."

"Why? So she'll feel guilty? It was a long time ago."

"But I think you're still carrying it, alone. You are not responsible for your family's happiness. They are all grown now and, if you didn't notice, very strong women.

Your father underestimated your mother. Is that why you joined the Army and now work in Oklahoma?"

"Eduardo wanted me to join with him, and it was a good way to provide for my family." It was easier for him to control his emotions if everyone was a phone call away instead of walking distance. That had included her and Sebastian. Pressing his palm against his forehead, he just wanted to go to bed and not think about the whys of his world. It was too complicated.

"You did a great job sharing with Cooper tonight. I was impressed. It's not the words that are going to stay with the boys as much as your actions. They will follow your example of what a man is."

He tilted his head back. "Great. No pressure."

"You're a good man, Bridges Espinoza."

"Eduardo should be here teaching them what it is to be a man." He regretted his words as soon as he saw the tears in her eyes.

"He's not here."

"Lilianna." He reached for her hand. How could he fix this?

"It's past my bedtime." She stretched, reaching for the sky. "So happy I get to sleep in tomorrow."

He followed her to her car for the second time tonight. "Text me."

She clicked her seatbelt, then looked up at him. The tears were gone. "Always the protector. Who gets to protect you?"

He ignored the last comment. "I won't go to bed until you text that you're safely tucked in with all your doors locked."

"Okay." She yawned. "But we are not done with this conversation."

He stood on his porch and watched her until the taillights faded into the darkness. Out of habit his instincts were telling him to run back to Oklahoma, but he couldn't uproot Cooper.

Did he really want to go back? His life had changed so much since the shooting. But if he wasn't a cop, who was he?

All the worrying might be all for nothing anyway. He was sure they wouldn't allowed to leave the state until the case was settled.

Unless Lilianna took full custody. Sebastian was his brother. He buried his fingers in his hair. A sharp pain pulled at his shoulder. *God, please give me guidance.* What would be the best for the people he loved?

Chapter Fourteen

It was almost noon as Lilianna stabbed a pastry. They sat outside under Panaderia de Dulces's colorful umbrellas. The bakery's patio was her favorite spot in town. Usually.

Across the street, the boys fished on the pier with Marguerite's husband and kids. Bridges had just returned from another PT session. In complete silence. Well, that wasn't true. He had answered a few questions with one-syllable words. He was more withdrawn than last week.

She had foolishly thought they had crossed some threshold last night, but it seemed he was more withdrawn than ever before. Her attempts to get into a deeper conversation were met with a stone wall. She was tired, and her emotions were all over the place. She hesitated to push him too hard because she knew he was in the same boat.

It had been a long night, and he didn't deal with emotions well. So much about him and their relationship had all fallen into place after she had heard what his father had done to him. At such a young age. Maybe he needed space.

This circle of thoughts didn't help either one of them. "Did I imagine our closeness last night?"

His gaze jerked from watching the boys to staring at her. "What? No."

"You're not talking to me. What's going on?"

He sat back and took a sip of his coffee. "Sorry. I'm trying to figure out what would be best for everyone. This morning I had a long talk with Sharon at CPS."

She leaned forward to make sure he got her full glare. "Did you think maybe I would want to be part of that discussion?"

Ignoring her hostility, he nodded. "Yeah. We're setting up an appointment. She suggested that we do a DNA test with Cooper, Sebastian and myself. That would prove family connections. Then we can talk about where he stays full-time."

Now she was confused. "I thought you were filing for full custody. Are there problems?"

"She thinks that, with bloodwork and our professions, we'll be able to settle things quickly. He doesn't have any family other than us." He sighed and finally looked at her. "Are we sure I'm the best place for him to be? When I go back to Oklahoma, I'll be back on the police force." He swirled the remains of his coffee in the cup and stared at it. "I want to make sure we are doing the best for him and Sebastian. I think Eduardo would want them together."

"You're overthinking and talking yourself in circles. I don't get it. Why are you pulling back from us?" Was she expecting too much? He had a life back in Oklahoma. "Do you have a time frame for returning to your job?"

He kept his head down, and after a while, she gave up on the idea that he would actually discuss with her what was going on in his mind.

With a sigh, he shifted in his chair. "I'm not sure. This would be so much easier if Eduardo was here. He should be the one taking care of Cooper and you. I'm sorry you're stuck with me."

Awareness dawned on her. She sat back in the chair and blew out a breath. She could hear the kids' laughter. "You have a point about the boys being good for each other. But we do need to talk about why you want to do this. I know you love both of them. I saw you with Cooper. You feel guilty. Eduardo made his choices." She leaned forward and took his hand. "You are not responsible for everyone. You can't be. It's impossible to do that and still have your own life."

He looked at his watch. "Are you sure about keeping Cooper for a couple more hours? I don't have to go with Sanchez to his meeting."

He was going to ignore her questions. "Yes. You're not listening to me, are you? I already told you that I'm taking them to see the groundwork for the maze. The boys would get a kick out of that. Then we're going to my house. You can join us there after your top-secret meeting and we can have dinner together. No matter what we decide to do, we need to explain to Sebastian how he has an older brother. Would you be there for that, please?"

"Of course, I'll be there. And it's not a top-secret meeting. Sanchez just asked for my input at the last minute. He's meeting with members of the city council and school board to talk about adding a resource officer on the school campus, with a K-9. I had some experience with that in Oklahoma."

Her heart rate jumped. "Is that something you could do here? Are you thinking about staying in Port Del Mar? Are they looking at hiring you?"

"No. It's not even a position yet. There's no funding. He just wants me there to help answer questions since I have firsthand experience. And this is the reason I didn't say anything. If my mom and sister found out, I wouldn't hear the end of it."

She reached for his hand. "I've been thinking of remaining here in Port Del Mar. I love working in the ER, but it takes so much of me. I can tell in the short time we've been in town that having me around more has made a difference with Sebastian. And now we have Cooper to consider."

He shifted. "What would you do?"

"I've been thinking of changing my focus to mommas and babies. The women's clinic where your sister works is getting ready to expand. She asked me if I was interested."

"I thought Savannah was a midwife in San Antonio."

"She is. But the group she works for is taking over a women's health clinic here, and she asked me to join her. I'd need some additional training. But I'm really thinking about it. I haven't missed San Antonio once. It's not that I didn't like it. I just feel like I'm home."

"You are." He glanced down. "I have to go."

"Go. I have Cooper, and I'll see you later at my house. We can talk about all this in more detail."

He got up and tucked some cash under his plate. He stopped to talk to the boys and then walked to the police station.

He might not be in the same place as she was. When she'd talked to Savannah about working here, she'd gotten excited. The idea of a new project here in Port Del Mar had her looking into the future and feeling hopeful about the possibilities. She wanted Bridges to see the possibilities too. She was feeling things for him that surprised her, but that wasn't enough if he just saw her as another responsibility.

There was so much she couldn't control but coming home put her where she needed to be. The only shadow in her heart was Bridges. She had a bad feeling that he'd never be able to see her as anything but Eduardo's widow.

She sighed. Eduardo. She tilted her head to stare at the white clouds that floated through the sky. Had he ever really loved her, or had she just been convenient?

Shaking her head, she looked for the boys. They were her focus. She was going to stay in Port Del Mar and raise her family.

Eduardo was gone, and Bridges was afraid of entanglements. The men in her life always walked away from her. She'd have to let Bridges go, just like she had let Eduardo go.

Since Eduardo had left on his last assignment, she had just been going through the motions, and she hadn't even realized it. She had a life to live, and two boys to raise. This time, she wasn't going to check out on all the new adventures.

She was on her own. That was fine. God had her.

Bridges paused at the white wooden gate leading to the backyard. The vacation-rental company had maintained the bungalow well.

But it called out for a family. While growing up here, Lilianna had told Eduardo and him that she planned to raise her children here, all six. They had laughed at her. They'd claimed they would never marry.

As he had gotten a little older, he had had visions of living here as her husband, with a couple of kids. But he had been too slow in sharing that with her. As usual, Eduardo had jumped in headfirst and claimed her as his. But Eduardo had been too restless to stay in Port Del Mar. He had wanted to see the world.

The boys' voices, raised in a mock battle, broke through his thoughts of the past. He smiled. He had so many wonderful memories of being in the backyard with Eduardo and Lilianna. Their lives had been so intertwined as kids. The boys needed that sense of family and belonging.

He leaned against the wall and listened to them as he looked to the sky. Why was he hanging out here instead of going in? It was no big deal; he'd eaten so many meals with Lilianna. But this one was different. He was having a hard time remembering his vow to Eduardo.

The kiss. Her touch. He was having a harder time keeping his distance.

Then she'd casually dropped a bomb on him with her announcement that she might move to Port Del Mar permanently. That had never occurred to him, and it had scrambled his brain.

He had thought about why it had affected him so much and what it meant for them long-term. So much so that he had been blindsided when Sanchez had mentioned that he would be perfect for the job.

The job. They already had the funding, but they weren't giving the program the go-ahead until they found a candidate they were confident in.

Bridges still hadn't really caught on until they were

leaving, and Sanchez had told him that he thought the interview had gone well and that they would know by next week. How had he missed that it had been an interview?

A job here in Port Del Mar, building a K-9 unit. So, without knowing it, he had lied to Lilianna. There was an opportunity here, but did he want to move back? His whole goal in life had been to leave Port Del Mar.

Staying here would solve so many problems—and create new ones.

And why was he standing here, hiding in the little grassy alleyway by her house? What he needed to do was go in and talk to Lilianna about this. She'd always been his go-to person when he had a decision to make. Of course, it was usually over the phone. Because that was safe.

Nothing with Lilianna was safe right now. That kiss had shifted his world. It had opened a box he had kept buried since they were sixteen. And now he wasn't sure how he would put all those feelings back in.

He looked to the truck knowing the picture was there, reminding him of the promise he'd made to his best friend. *Eduardo, you messed up on so many levels. You know that, right? I thought my days of cleaning up your troubles were over. This is not fair to Lilianna or your boys.*

Mack whined and put his paw on the gate. "Okay. Enough with the overthinking." He pushed open the gate and heard the boys' laughter. They were good for each other. Separating them would be difficult—and possibly hurtful.

He couldn't imagine not seeing Cooper every morning over breakfast. He'd gotten used to starting his day off that way. Hauling Cooper all the way to Oklahoma, away from the family connections he was just now building, wouldn't be fair to the kid either.

This position that Sanchez was trying to lure him into might be a gift from God when it came to what Cooper needed. But it was less pay, and he would be moving home to deal with his family on a daily basis instead of via phone calls.

And he would see Lilianna every day.

"Tío Bridges!" Sebastian waved from the tree house. Big Mack barked at his side. He patted the dog. "Go on." In a flash, the dog was up in the tree house.

He stood under the giant oak branches. "Where's Cooper?"

Sebastian put his finger to his mouth. He looked over his shoulder. "We're planning a sneak attack on the pirates that have been stealing all the dogs in town. Do you want to play with us? You could be the pirate. We have a sword."

"Maybe later. Right now, I'm looking for your mom." They had a lot to talk about, and with the boys playing outside, this would be a good time.

"She's in the house. Earlier she let us rescue her, even though she said she was capable of saving herself and us. She said next time she gets to be Wonder Woman." He grinned. "Then she said she had to go clean dishes. I don't think superheroes do dishes."

"Your super mom does whatever she wants." Cooper came up to the edge of the tree house and looked over the wall. "We saw where they're putting the maze. It's so big. Seeing it in real life is the coolest thing that has ever happened to me."

"You both did a really job. I can't wait to walk through it."

Cooper grabbed Sebastian's shoulder. "Come on. I'll show you the traps I set." The boys disappeared into their imaginary world.

Stepping through the back door, he heard music he recognized from their high school days. It was one of the songs they would sing along with when they cruised up and down the beach. A new piece came on, and Bridges knew immediately that it was the one that had been playing when the wedding picture he kept was taken.

He stopped at the edge of the kitchen. Should he back out and go play with the boys? What if she wasn't as okay as she'd acted this morning? She usually took everything in stride, but this was a huge hit to the heart. It would make sense if she needed more time.

He could sneak out and text her that he'd picked up the boys and that she could take as much time as she needed. No, that was just making it easier on him. With a sigh, he stepped forward.

There might be something he could do to help. Going into the living room, he spotted her in the reading nook to the left. She was curled up in the overstuffed floral chair. Her head was down, a curtain of hair hanging to her shoulder, hiding her face.

The backyard was visible through the floor-to-ceiling windows lining the rear wall. Sunshine softly caressed the room. She tucked the fallen hair behind her ear, and he saw the soft curves of her face highlighted by the natural glow. The tension eased from his body. He wanted to sink into the pillows surrounding her. He could stand there and stare at her all day. Engrossed in whatever she was reading, she had no clue he was there.

He frowned. That wasn't safe.

Taking one step forward, he then paused, hesitant to

interrupt her. He needed to do something, at some point staring at her would start to get creepy. "Lilianna?"

With a sharp shriek, she jumped. She put her hand to her chest. "Bridges, you scared me. What are you doing sneaking up on people like that?"

The impact of her direct stare locked his chest. He had no business longing to hold her. Ugh. He was losing control of his resolve. "It's not safe to be unaware of your surroundings. You never heard me enter the house." Great. Now he was yelling at her.

She frowned at him in confusion. "You're giving me a safety lecture?"

"No." He hovered at the entryway between the living room and the kitchen. "Sorry. I didn't mean to startle you."

"I was so deep in thought that a hurricane could have knocked the house down around me." She smiled at him. "Come." She scooted over and patted the spot next to her.

Was it an oversize chair or a loveseat? He shuddered at the word. Whatever it was, he was better off standing. Awkwardly, in the doorway. Yeah, that was a stupid plan.

"Join me. I want to show you what I found."

"Are you okay?" He didn't move. He took his time to study her. She didn't look upset. "You want me to leave and go out back with the boys?"

"No. I have enchiladas in the oven. They'll be done in thirty minutes." Tilting her head, she closed one eye and pursed her lips. "What's going on? Are you okay?"

"Yeah." He wanted to groan out loud. That was too fast, and his voice had gone all high-pitched.

She laughed. She really did appear relaxed. It was a

relief to see that she wasn't falling apart. There was actually a peaceful air about her. He stepped into the room but didn't sit down. "What are you doing?"

"I left a box of stuff from high school and college in the attic. There are tons of letters from Eduardo when y'all were in Georgia. Some from you too." She looked down and traced the edge of the paper in her lap. "I've always kept with me the last letter he wrote. It arrived two days after they told me he was dead." She held out her hand to him.

He sat down next to her and pulled her close. "You didn't tell me."

"I couldn't look at it without crying. It's my last piece of him, but I haven't read it in a while." Gently, she folded it and looked up at him, her eyes dry. "He loved me."

"Of course, he did."

With a nod, she sighed and laid her head on his shoulder. "Whatever happened twelve years ago with Cooper's mom wasn't a part of our marriage. In some of the older letters, I do see loneliness and guilt. There was even one where we talked about going our separate ways. That must've been when he was seeing her." She tapped the folded letter against her chest. "This letter is nothing but love."

"I never doubted for a second that he loved you with his whole heart. You, Sebastian and the Army were his life."

She grinned. "Not always in that order."

"No. But he was loyal." He slipped an arm around her. "Every time we talked, it was all about you and Sebastian. He could spend hours talking about how amazing it was that you loved him and he didn't understand how he deserved you."

She scoffed. "He was something else. That was for sure." She stood up and went to the white built-in shelves. A pretty blue box sat with its lid off. She gently laid the letter inside, closed the lid and patted the top. "It's time this letter went with the others. Maybe Sebastian or even Cooper will want to read them. I don't want anger to cloud the good memories. We had a solid marriage, and I want the boys to know that. All those negative emotions are too heavy to live with."

Bridges nodded. "We both know life is way too short to carry all the bad garbage." Breaking eye contact with her, he watched as the boys jumped from the tree house to run up the ladder again. "I see Cooper as an extra blessing. I love that kid more than I ever thought possible."

She curled back into her chair, tucking her feet underneath her. She looked out the window. "He is. Did you know I had finally convinced Eduardo that it was time for a second child?"

"It was a hot topic with him. He had finally given in? I'm sorry."

"No. It's good. I hated being an only child, and I didn't want that for Sebastian. We'd decided that when Eduardo came home, we would start working on that second baby." A half laugh, half snort escaped her. "Leave it to Eduardo to find such a creative way of giving me my second child."

"Once he made a promise, he did keep it." He looked from the boys to her. "We have a lot to be grateful for. It can be easy to forget that."

She turned from the window and studied him for a long second.

He shifted his weight. "What?"

She rested her jaw on her palm. "Why haven't you ever married?"

He blinked a couple of times, processing her question. How to answer that? Silence was easier.

For a while. Then it got awkward. Sweat formed around his neck. His whole body went hot. He should stand and get some distance, but he didn't. "Now you sound like my mom and sisters. You've been hanging out with them too much."

She swatted at his arm, then left her hand there. The warmth seeped through the thin layer of cotton. "Bridges, really. You have so much to offer. And you'd be the best dad. I don't understand why you've always been single. If you've dated anyone, you never mentioned her."

"I've never met anyone that fit into my life or that I liked enough to change my life." He shrugged. "Not everyone is meant to be in a relationship."

They sat in silence for a while, but then she shifted and took his hand. "There's no one in Oklahoma? Aren't you lonely?"

"Better lonely than miserable with the wrong person." He fed her the old line he always gave his family.

She cupped his face and leaned in. The scent of her, fresh flowers and summer, surrounded him.

"I'm okay, Lilianna. My family is good, and if you're happy, that's all I need."

"No. You deserve more." She scooted closer. "You're my best friend, but I think we could be more."

His heart slammed against his chest, and the pressure pushed against his ears. He couldn't think or speak. There were no words in his brain.

She made a sweet sound that might have been some sort of a laugh. "You look as if I'd said you had six months to live." She bit her bottom lip and sat back.

Distance. Yes, that's what he needed. He should stand and…and…what? What should he do with that statement? She wanted more from him? He was still sitting next to her. Why didn't his body move?

"Bridges. Please tell me what's going on in your head. I'm feeling a little exposed here. This isn't a spur-of-the-moment decision. I've been thinking about you—and us—for weeks now. We kissed, and it meant something. Didn't it?"

He couldn't take the self-doubt that now burned in her eyes. "Emotions were high. You've always been important to me. So, yes. It meant something, but it can't be more."

"Why not?"

"I can't step into Eduardo's life and take what should be his." He couldn't look at her, but she deserved his honesty. "Lilianna, more importantly than that, I can't risk losing your friendship. Whatever you feel for me might just be all the weird emotions from dealing with Eduardo having a son."

"I loved Eduardo. But I'm not going to put the rest of my life on hold for him. I have to live without him. He was a huge part of who I am today, but that doesn't mean my life stopped with his."

"I know. But what if you're just confused?" He looked to the kitchen. "I should go check on the boys." He couldn't move away from her. Could she be his?

No. He had to protect them all. Eduardo was dead. He

couldn't take over his friend's life, no matter how much he wanted to. It would be self-serving, and she deserved a man of true honor. "I'm not Eduardo."

And he couldn't replace him. He stood, but he couldn't go far. The blue box with the letter inside was at eye level. Next to it was a picture of Eduardo in his uniform, holding a baby Sebastian. Behind all that was a folded flag in a wooden case. The flag that had covered him on the trip home. "I'm not Eduardo." He repeated.

Chapter Fifteen

Lilianna wanted to go to him and wrap her arms around him—or maybe pound some sense into him. He looked so alone, and it was his own fault. "I know that. You're so different from Eduardo. Over the last month, my feelings for you have started to change." She pressed her lips together. Everything in her wanted to tell him she was falling in love with him. But if she was reading the room right, it was too soon for him to hear that word from her. Maybe too soon for both of them.

He braced his hand on the shelf and had a staring contest with Eduardo's photo. "I can't do this."

Lilianna stared at him. "You can't do what? See me as a romantic partner? You can't love me?" Her core went numb. She wanted to take that back. It had sounded so pathetic. And after she had just told herself not to use that word. "I'm sorry."

"Don't be." He made a harsh sound that might have been a laugh. "No." He shook his head. "Loving you is easy…too easy." His knuckles turned white as his grip tightened on the edge of the board. He leaned in closer to the photo. "I also love Eduardo, and I can't betray him. You're his."

The churning in her gut sparked. "You really believe that if I love again, I'm betraying Eduardo? I have to be alone for the rest of my life because he died too young?"

"No." A frustrated-sounding grunt came from him as he interlocked his fingers on the top of his head. "That's not what I meant. It just can't be me."

She moved to stand in front of him, to force him to look her in the eyes and break whatever weird connection he was having with the photo. "You're okay if I date Officer Sanchez? He asked me out. Or there's Pastor Rod. Everyone keeps telling me he's single. Some people have even mentioned we'd make a good match."

His jaw clenched and he looked away.

Tears burned her eyes. "You do think I should stay Eduardo's widow for the next fifty or sixty years. Never having more kids. All the while I get to see you married and start your own—"

"No!" Anger flared in his eyes. "You, Sebastian and Cooper are my family. The only family I want." He moved away from her. "The boys are our priority right now."

"I'm so confused. If we're your family, then why can't you and I be more?"

Standing at the window, he braced an arm against the frame above his head. "You and the boys are the most important people in my world. Why would we put that in jeopardy for some fleeting romance?"

Self-imposed isolation and loneliness radiated off him. Moving behind him, she gave into the urge to wrap an arm around his waist and lay her cheek on the back of his shoulder.

He stiffened for a second, then put his other hand on top of hers. "It's your happiness that matters the most." His voice was low and hoarse. "I have to protect that above all else."

Her eyes burned, and she hugged him closer for a minute before replying. "What if you are my happiness?"

His head dropped. "Please don't do this to me."

Pressing her face closer, she took a deep breath. She would not cry. Nope. He was security, love and stability, but he wasn't hers if he didn't want the same thing she wanted. She dropped her arm and stepped away from his warmth. "I'm sorry. Is it too painful to be around us? Is that the problem? You miss Eduardo that much?"

"I do miss him." He turned to her. "But that's not the issue. Being happy with you because he died seems wrong." He moved to the next shelf, where she had several pictures of Eduardo and Sebastian. "If he were alive, you would have never noticed me in a…" He looked to the ceiling. "Romantic way."

Leaving the window, she stood next to him. She touched her favorite photo of Eduardo and Sebastian. There were some of Eduardo and Bridges too. She made a mental note to add some of Cooper. "You've always been in my life, and you're right. But Eduardo isn't here, so why can't our feelings change and grow into something else? It seems very natural to me."

He was breathing hard and making a point not to look at her. She wanted to reach out and soothe all his pain, but he was stiff and unapproachable. "Bridges. This is new territory for both of us. We can take it slow."

"It's not new to me." He fixed his concentration on a picture of the three of them, before she'd had Sebastian.

Picking it up, he stared at it. "I fell so hard in love with you a long time ago. Before Eduardo said anything."

Her brain couldn't process what he'd said, and her chest tightened. "I don't understand. There's never been anything between us until now."

With a grimace, he replaced the picture. He flashed her a smile, but it didn't reach his eyes. His focus going back to the photographs, he picked up the one from their wedding.

"I know my feelings were all one-sided, and once Eduardo announced his love for you in the middle of the football field during halftime, I made sure to not feel them. To bury my love so deep it would never see the light of day. You were happy with him and he adored you. At sixteen, I hadn't had the nerve to speak up, and the braver man won you. How do I undo all those years of denial?"

He left the reading nook and went to the living room and looked around like he was lost and searching for the exit.

She had never heard so much pain in his voice before. "You were always there with us."

"I loved you both, and like I said earlier, your happiness was all that mattered. You had chosen Eduardo, and I respected your relationship. There was no way I could let either one of you know I had ever loved you. So, I didn't. I cut it out of my life."

"He's not here anymore."

He shook his head and went to the kitchen, then back to the living room. "Don't you get it? You had each other. I should be the one dead. He…he…" His gaze darted around the room as if the words he searched for were hiding behind the furniture. "I've loved you so long that it feels like a betrayal if I act on it now that he's gone."

He buried his fingers in his hair. "I should have been with him. He had wanted me to reenlist with him. But I told him no. The first time I refused him, and you end up a widow. I should have been there to look out for him. Sebastian and Cooper would have their real father. I can't just step in and replace him."

"Bridges. That's not even logical. You probably wouldn't have been stationed together."

"I didn't say the guilt was rational."

The instinct to hold him and comfort him was too strong to deny. She entangled her arm with his and rested her head on his shoulder. "I don't know what to say or do. But you know you've always been my best friend, and the thought of you hurting this way is tearing me up. Eduardo would not want this torment for you."

His profile was so strong. "You've always been the one that took care of us." She gently touched his chin and brought his tortured gaze to hers. "You're right. This is new to me. Let's eat. Tell the boys crazy stories about Eduardo and take it one day at a time. We're still friends, right?"

He nodded and sat down on the sofa. "I came here today so we could explain to Sebastian that Cooper is really his brother."

She could see him compartmentalizing his emotions. Her eyes and throat burned with tears she could not shed in front of him. He was too good at pushing down his feelings.

The timer went off in the kitchen. "Dinner's ready. Would you get the boys and make sure they wash up?"

He was up already, a little too eager to have such a

mundane task. Would he ever be able to let the guilt go and allow them to be more than friends?

Was she expecting too much? But it broke her heart in completely new ways when she thought of him alone. She loved Bridges.

With a smile, she flopped back on the cushions. After Eduardo's death, she couldn't imagine ever having that type of relationship again. But now she knew she could. The heart was a marvelous gift from God.

Bridges might not ever be able to return her love, but she wasn't broken. If Bridges didn't want her heart, she could find someone else one day. The timer went off again, and she rushed to the kitchen before dinner was ruined.

Pulling out the casserole, she went to the refrigerator to get the salad and bread.

She turned up the music and danced. She was capable of loving again, and there were no limits or timers to beat.

The boys rushed in as she was setting the table. They held up their hands. "All clean, Mom!"

"Good job."

Just having them in the room lifted the energy, and she had to smile. Halfway through the meal, she made eye contact with Bridges and he nodded.

"Guys, we found out some really cool information. Cooper knows all about it."

She smiled. "I think you'll like this, Sebastian. What did you ask me for on your last birthday and Christmas?"

Sebastian looked confused. "But you said you couldn't give me a brother." His eyes went big. "Is Cooper going to live with us full-time?" He bounced in his chair. "We can share a room. I have a bunk bed."

"Hold on, Champ." Bridges put his hand on Cooper's shoulder. The boy had gone still, staring at his plate. "What we recently found out was that Cooper's mom knew your dad, way before your parents were married. You and Cooper have the same father."

Sebastian's eyes went big. "What does that mean?" He turned to Cooper.

"You're brothers." She patted Cooper's hand.

Cooper nodded, but worry marked his face.

Sebastian rushed Lilianna and hugged her. "Thank you."

She put her arms around him and hugged him tight. The tough questions might come later, but for right now, she was completely grateful for a seven-year-old's innocence.

"I want him to live with us."

"He'll live with Bridges, but he's our family and we're his. Let's finish dinner. I have a surprise cobbler waiting for us."

"With ice cream?" Sebastian asked.

"Of course." She blinked back the tears. This was all she needed for now. Two happy boys at her table.

The morning sun had climbed high and turned the air hot and humid as Bridges slipped the halter off the horse he had been riding. It had been a good morning working with the horses and dogs.

Damian turned the last horse out to pasture. "Thanks, guys, for helping me put mileage on them. I get twice as much work done when you're here. Goldie is ready to head home." He pointed to the palomino mare Bridges had been riding.

Cooper climbed the fence and leaned over with his hand out to scratch the horse's jaw. "She likes this. I'll miss her. If I was you, I'd be sad all the time if I couldn't keep them."

"She has people that love her and are waiting for her. I take care of them long enough for them to get where they need to be in order to be happy with their families. When they go home, it means I have room to help more."

"You're like a foster home for messed-up horses and dogs. The good kind of foster home. That's cool. Can I take Beast through the obstacle course one more time?" He grinned. "Or two."

The labradoodle sat and wagged his tail, knowing they were talking about him. Cooper kneeled in front of the big dog. Damian nodded. "Sure."

"Just twice," Bridges told him. "Then we're going to the cabin to fix lunch."

"Are Lilianna and Sebastian coming over?"

"Not today. It's just us." Saturday had rattled his world, and he had enough self-awareness to know he was avoiding Lilianna. Her wanting more from him was hard to process.

Cooper's shoulders slumped. "Okay. I wish we could ride every day. Do you think we could let Sebastian join us?"

"Sure. Later this week." Damian turned to Bridges. "I could bring one of the trail horses up."

Cooper ran toward the course, followed by four big dogs.

"That's really a good kid you got there." Damian leaned his back on the gate and watched Cooper.

Bridges nodded, his heart tightening at the thought of everything the boy had been through, and yet he still managed to trust them. He hoped he wouldn't do anything to destroy the bond they had built. "He's pretty amazing, considering everything he's had to deal with in twelve short years."

Gathering the halters, Damian walked to the barns. "Thanks for helping me work with the horses. I'm able to see the progress moving faster. Which means I can get them home quicker. Or work with more animals."

"There's a peace about being focused on a horse or dog that's hard to find anywhere else. It takes me back to the good days with my dad, before he got sick. It's the best part of coming home."

"Speaking of home…" Damian went into the tack room to organize the leads and halters. "Have you given much more thought about the job offer in town?" he called from inside.

"It just seems too perfect to be true." Bridges stood at the barn door and watched Cooper guide the dog through the obstacle course. "But I never saw myself settling here."

Damian joined him. "It may be selfish of me, but I'm really hoping that you stay. With Lexy traveling, I want the freedom to go with her, which means I need someone I can trust to make sure the animals stay on schedule. I need to hire someone part-time, but I haven't found anyone I trust. Belle's too busy for me to always rely on her. The barn can hold twice as many horses as I keep now. I could build bigger dog kennels if I had the right partner." He was looking at his boots. "I'd like to expand the rescue training, which would tie in with you organizing a new K-9 unit for Port Del Mar. What do you think?"

"You want *me* to help you expand?"

Damian sighed and looked to where his dogs sat watching Cooper and Beast. "Yes. You. Everything you want is here. Horses, dogs, Cooper, Sebastian and Lilianna."

He knew that Damian didn't make this offer lightly. His mind rolled all the possibilities over in his head. But that would mean he would permanently move back home. Did he really want to do that?

Cooper laughed and rubbed the labradoodle behind the ears. Bridges's chest tightened. He could be here for all the little moments in Cooper and Sebastian's lives. He would also see Lilianna every day.

"Usually, I try to avoid giving advice to anyone, but I have firsthand experience with thinking I don't deserve people in my life. But it came to my attention that my idea of protecting them was counterproductive and making us all miserable. Don't overthink it. Just go to God and move in the direction that spreads the love." Damian smirked. "Consider who this is coming from. I, Damian De La Rosa, just said to spread the love. That's how good my life is right now, because I took the risk and let Lexy care for me."

Bridges's stubbornness and deliberations were making everything worse. Maybe it was time to get over himself.

"Uh-oh." Damian was looking over Bridges's shoulder. "Someone's in trouble."

When he turned, Bridges saw his mother's little truck bouncing over the cattle guard. He groaned. Damian patted him on the back. "Can't be good if Momma Espinoza is tracking you down. Time for me to go." He headed to the courses.

After stepping out of her vehicle, his mom waved and charged straight for him.

"*Mijo*, where have you been? I was getting worried, so I came out to check on you."

He sighed. This was one of the reasons he lived in Oklahoma. "I saw you Sunday at church, then I hung out at your house for three hours afterward."

"That was three days ago." She hugged him and patted his cheek. "Why have you not told me about the offer Andres gave you? Setting up a K-9 unit as a school resource officer sounds perfect, and much safer than your job all the way up north."

"I'm pretty sure no one considers Oklahoma 'up north.' You know it's actually connected to Texas, right?" He kissed her on the cheek. "How did you hear about the offer?" Why was he even pretending there was any sort of privacy in this small town?

"I know people. I was waiting for you to come and ask my advice, but you didn't." Her glare took him back to being a six-year-old caught stealing tortillas before dinner.

"Sorry. I was just processing all the reasons to stay or to go back."

Cooper and Big Mack joined them. His mom patted the dog and told him what a pretty boy he was, then she turned to Cooper. She grabbed his chin. "Look at you. You've gotten taller since the last time I saw you. You're growing up too fast. I need bricks for your head." She kissed him on the cheek.

"*Que está pasando?*" Bridges knew that his question sounded more like an accusation. He sighed. "Mom. Why are you here?"

"I came to feed my newest grandson." She kissed Cooper on the head. "Another year, and he's going to be taller than me."

Cooper's panicked gaze darted to Bridges. "You didn't tell her?"

She looked between them, confused. "Tell me what, *mijo*?"

"I'm not his son." He dropped his head as if he were hiding from rejection or shame.

"Oh, that." She swatted at the air, then lifted his chin until they were eye to eye. "He told me that long ago, but it doesn't change the fact that he says you're his son. You're my grandson and I'm your *abuelita*." She laid her hand on her chest, then grabbed him and kissed him on the forehead again. "I brought *fideo*. It was your father's favorite when he was growing up. Come help me. I have sweets too. Not the leftovers from the bakery but made just for you."

They sat on the cabin's back porch and ate. Cooper asked for seconds, cleaning two bowlfuls. Finishing his, Bridges sat back. He did love his mother's cooking. Well, he loved her too.

"Is it okay if I go up and play my game?"

"As soon as you put the dishes away and thank your *abuelita*."

Cooper hugged her. "*Gracias*, Abuelita. You're the best cook." After collecting the now-empty bowls, he hurried inside.

She put her rocker in motion. "Now tell me what is going on with you?"

Couldn't a man sulk in peace? "You seem to know everything already, so why ask me?"

She glared at him from the corner of her eye. How did she do that?

"Because something is troubling you. I know my children. Explain. We will talk through it, and God will show us the way. Have you been praying?"

"Yes." He closed his eyes. "Maybe not as much as I should."

"Every morning and night I lift my children up in prayer. Everything I would wish for you is at your door, but you are still talking about running away."

"Mom, I'm pretty sure a thirty-one-year-old going back to work is not running away."

She shook her head. "Lies can eat away at your happiness. They grow in the dark. So, stop lying to me and tell me what is really going on."

He leaned forward and braced his elbows on his knees. "I'm not lying. I just have hard decisions to make."

"Why are they so hard? Everything you could want is right here." She scooted to the edge of her chair and patted his arm. "Just stay."

She was so little, but her faith was so big. "How did you do it? It had to be beyond hard to raise all seven kids on your own. My sisters tested you every step of the way when they went through their teen years. And you took in anyone that needed a home, a mother. And with Reno's disappearance… How?"

"When Reno went missing for a week—" she clasped her hands tightly in her lap "—that almost did me in, but your sisters and you were so brave and lifted me up. I was never alone. God brought people into my life that stood tall in faith when I couldn't. God had me and He had Reno. I don't know why we were spared the worst. But God was always with me. Just like when I lost your father so suddenly."

"But you just keep going. Nothing fazes you."

"Oh, that's not true. In the shower or late at night when I'd reach over and find the bed empty, I would cry buckets. That's why I let the girls start sleeping with me. Once I got Reno back, I was so focused on him, the poor baby couldn't breathe. But we all got through the worst, and we have each other. Why are you thinking about that?"

"I'm a father now, and I have to put Cooper's needs ahead of mine."

"That boy belongs here with family. Lilianna is staying. I would think that alone would make you want to remain."

He did not want to talk to his mother about Lilianna. "It's not so easy."

"Why not? You love her. You always have." She leaned forward and lowered her voice. "I think she might be falling in love with you. You should settle here. Together you'd make the most beautiful couple."

"That's part of the problem. She's Eduardo's widow." He looked out across the pasture. "Should you be going home now?"

Sitting back, she glared at him. "You might be more stubborn than your father."

"What? How does me wanting to protect the people I love make me stubborn?"

"Thinking you have to carry all the burdens. Do I look fragile to you? Does Lilianna? She works in a big-city ER. That girl knows how to take care of herself.

She was married to Eduardo. That alone proved how strong that girl is. That boy was a mess. Jumping without thinking anything through. You cleaned up his messes. What does her being Eduardo's widow have to do with having a relationship with her now? It's not like he died last week."

"Mom!"

"I loved that boy as much as I love my own kids, but he lived as long as he did because you were there to save him."

"I should have been there. With him." He looked away. "Sorry, Mom. I didn't mean that. It just makes loving Lilianna complicated."

"Oh, *mijo*." She moved next to him and cupped his face. "That type of guilt is just a waste of time. It was out of your hands, and nothing can change the past. Don't waste the opportunity to make wonderful memories because of pride." She rested her forehead on his. "I loved your father. But don't make the mistakes he made."

"Mistakes?" He didn't see the connection.

"Do you know that he was sick for a year before he told me? It was only after I finally tricked him with a doctor appointment that he confessed he was dying. We had three weeks left. Three weeks." She sat back down but didn't let go of his hand. "Why would he do that to me? That whole time, sneaking around to doctors behind my back. He spent extra hours on the ranch to settle things and to avoid me seeing the truth." Tears clouded her eyes, and she wiped at them. "There were treatments he could have done. But he didn't even talk it over with me. We could have had more time or at least made special memories. He thought I was too weak to know. So, he suffered alone, without telling anyone, and stole so much from us in the name of protecting his family."

The wind rustled the tall grass, and birds called out. Bridges took his mother's hand. "He told me."

She went very still. "What do you mean? When did he tell you?"

"When he first found out. About a year before he died. I had to help at the ranch when he couldn't do certain things. He said we had to protect you and the girls. Reno was too little. It was our job to make sure you were happy."

She blinked back tears, but this time, they fell.

"Mommy, don't cry. I should have told you. I'm sorry we lied."

"Hush. It's not your fault." Her finger touched his lips. "He had no business putting that burden on you. You've carried that all these years. Oh, *mijo*. We're not meant to carry the weight of grief alone as adults. I can't even imagine the struggle you went through as a child. I'm so sorry I didn't notice."

It broke his heart that they had hurt his mother in any way. "Please, don't blame yourself."

Leaning in, she hugged him as if he were a small boy again and she could remove all the pain with a kiss. "God gifted us with families to share the burden. You are more like your father than I thought."

She sat back but kept a firm grip on his hands. "Don't you understand that it would have been a gift to care for your father and go on that journey with him for as long as I could?" Shifting, she studied the sky, then looked back at him. "Stop trying to carry us all. We are strong enough to deal with life. Don't underestimate us like your father did. Don't steal the gifts God meant for you to share with Lilianna and the boys. You're not protecting them. You're just shielding your own heart because you don't want to see them in pain. And in doing so, you are missing out on some of the most beautiful memories." She released a hand and wiped a tear off his cheek.

When had he started crying? He never cried.

"When it's all said and done, it's the memories we leave with our loved ones."

"Mom. I'm not sure I can let go of everything and love her like she deserves."

"You're scared. It's okay. But don't let fear hold you from the life God meant for you to have. I love you, and I release you from the promises that your father had you make. You are not responsible for our happiness. What if you are Lilianna's happiness?"

He frowned. "Did she tell you that?"

"No. She hasn't spoken about you. I tried, but she'll talk only about anything else."

"She said that to me. When I was giving her reasons why we shouldn't be together, she gave me one reason we should."

Tapping him on the head, she gave him her best mom's-not-messing-around glare. "Why are we having this discussion? Stop being *estupido*. Go claim your future."

While he was still trying to process everything, they had just talked about, she stood up and went inside. He followed and found her at the base of the ladder. "*Mijo!* Come down and give your Abuelita a kiss goodbye."

He stood, an irrational panic surging through his system. "You're leaving?"

Cooper and Mack joined them. Yolanda kissed Cooper's cheek, then patted it. "Be a good boy and grab my dishes and take them to the truck."

"Yes, ma'am. I mean, Abuelita."

With a pleased smile, she watched him hurry to do as she asked. "I'm leaving because we are done talking. It is time for doing. You are good at that, so go and fix this."

"What if it's too late? I… How do I fix this?" What if Lilianna didn't really love him the way he loved her?

She marched outside, not even giving him any of her looks. With her hand on the railing, she looked at him. "You've loved her all her life. You know what to do. Trust that God has already given you everything you need." And with that, she was gone. After avoiding his mother for so many years, he felt lost.

Cooper came back with Mack. "Everything okay?" He looked worried. There was still so much uncertainty in the boy's life.

"It will be." His body relaxed. "It will be." As soon as he told Lilianna he loved her.

Chapter Sixteen

It was unusually cool for a July morning, but Lilianna knew that by the time the sun hit the midpoint in the sky, it would be humid and sticky.

But for now, everything was shiny and green, high-lighted by the red, white and blue that covered the town. Summerfest by the Sea had always been the largest event in Port Del Mar.

Lilianna waved and smiled at the familiar faces of people she had grown up with. They were older but still so familiar. A good number had already heard about her taking the job at the new women's health clinic and were congratulating her. Why had she stayed away so long?

"Mom! Look!" Sebastian had a small watermelon in his arms. The float with the sea turtles was passing them out. "How awesome, right? Angie got one too."

The kids had a ton of brightly colored red, white and blue plastic necklaces draped all over them. Cooper laughed as another group passing them drenched everyone with powerful water guns.

Damian's mounted rescue team was ending the parade. Her heart skipped as Bridges came into view. He smiled and waved to people lining the streets.

She didn't even fight the compulsion to stare at him. He was so natural on the horse, his black cowboy hat so low that all she could make out was the lower part of his face.

He smiled at someone. Would he ever smile at her again, or had she ruined it with her request of wanting more from him?

Behind the horses was Officer Sanchez, indicating the end of the parade. The town of four hundred people now had four thousand people making their way to the plaza and boardwalk.

Bridges stopped his horse next to them. The big roan was not bothered by the crowds. Some of the tourists took pictures. He wasn't looking at her. Instead, he was grinning at Sebastian and Cooper.

"Did y'all have a good time?"

"We got candy, water bottles and watermelons. Even a bag of oranges. It was so much fun. I wish we could've ridden the horses with you."

"We'll get you and Cooper some practice, so maybe next year." He dismounted. "Why don't you get on and you can ride double to the trailer? You can help rub down the horses and load them up. I'm pretty sure Damian wants out of here as fast as possible." He finally looked at her. "Is it okay if I take them? I know how much you love the booths at the arts-and-crafts show. Eduardo and I never let you stay too long." He grinned. "Sorry about that."

Did he just smile at her? But he was still thinking of her with Eduardo. She sighed. "One of the drawbacks with having two best friends who were boys."

"I can't do anything about your taste back then, but I can give you a little freedom from mom duty now. So, go take your time, and we'll meet you at my sisters' truck in the food-truck area. No rush—whenever you're ready. I think there'll be enough snacks to keep these two busy for a while."

"Don't let them eat too much. They'll get sick."

He looked confused. "I thought that was the goal at a fair?"

She rolled her eyes. "Do not let them challenge each other to any weird food-eating contests. You and Eduardo were sick for days. He never could eat whole jalapeños again. Just the sight of them made him turn green."

Bridges laughed. "He did that all on his own. I told him not to do it, but you know what happened when someone threw down a dare. He was all over it. Go have fun supporting local artists and visiting." He kissed her on the cheek, then helped the boys onto the roan and walked away like he just hadn't thrown a grenade into the middle of her nice little day.

What was going on?

Lilianna held her hand on the spot he had kissed. Her skin still tingled as her three favorite people in the world rode away from her. She had definitely made the right decision to stay in Port Del Mar.

Her good mood dampened. When would he be leaving? It had to be soon, because she'd been here a month.

Walking through the booths, she browsed handmade pottery, jewelry and some amazing wood crafts. She smiled and chatted, but Bridges wasn't far from her mind.

Arms loaded with bags full of handcrafted items, she made her way to the food trucks. Bridges was going to have to make his decisions, and she would make hers. No matter what happened, she was no longer just going through the motions. She was living her full life. With or without Bridges. She groaned. It would be so much better with him.

Regardless, though, she was going to enjoy her blessings and be happy here. Life was too short for anything else.

The Espinozas' truck had a long line, but the sisters, with the help of a few other family members, served everyone quickly and with a smile. They were selling empanadas and churros as a fundraiser.

Reno was just stepping into the truck with a large, covered pan. "The cheesy-beef empanadas are flying today." He winked at Lilianna.

Once he was in, Marguerite came out. She hugged Lilianna. "You've been shopping. I was about to go buy some of the candied pecans."

"Do you need help in the truck?"

"Over the years, we've worked out a system. Routine and schedule make the work easier and fun. If we mess it up—" her hand went into the air "—total chaos. Where's that brother of mine? And the boys?" She looked around her eyes wide. "You're all alone."

"He's with the kids, putting up the horses."

Josefina and Savannah came out of the truck and hugged her.

Savannah kept an arm around her. "I'm so excited you took Dr. Hernandez's offer. We'll get to work together. The guys are in command for the next hour, so we can go shopping. That's the plan, but I doubt these two will stay away that long." She pointed to Marguerite and Josefina.

"I give it thirty minutes," Reno yelled from the back of the food truck.

Marguerite rolled her eyes. "I said an hour." She looked at her phone. "Fifty minutes now. You want to join us?"

"No thanks. I've done my share of stimulating the local economy. I'm waiting for Bridges and the boys."

Josefina clicked her tongue. "What's *mijo*'s problem? Everyone in town knows that he's been offered that job. He just needs to take it. My mom must've dropped him on his head way too many times as a baby."

Her stomach dipped. He hadn't said anything about the offer. The idea that he wasn't talking to her hurt.

Lips in a tight line, Marguerite nodded. "He has the perfect job and you—" she waved at Lilianna "—right here. What else would he want?"

Reno stuck his head out the door. "Maybe sisters that don't stick their noses in his business. You're running out of time. Stop trying to run Bridges's life and go socialize or shop or whatever you do when you aren't being bossy."

"You have customers, Reno." Marguerite put her hands on her hips. "Bridges has a way of making everything more complicated than it needs to be. He thinks too much. He has to think about it and then think about what he thought about."

Josefina crossed her arms and huffed. "He's gonna waste his whole life thinking about it."

Reno poked his head out again and frowned at them. "Ladies! I'm not sure I'm using that term correctly, but you won't be solving all of Bridges's problems today. Go. You'll run out of time."

The three sisters left, still complaining about their brother.

His being analytical and thoughtful in his actions and words was one of the reasons she loved Bridges. He didn't charge into a situation, then change his mind when it didn't work out the way he wanted.

If he moved back to Oklahoma, it would mean that he had thought about it and didn't see a future for them together.

"Mom!" Sebastian came running. "Look!" He held up his arm and a bright green glob of goo slid down it, changing colors as it went. He caught it with his other hand. "Isn't this cool?"

"So cool." She just hoped it didn't stain.

Cooper had mustard on his face from the German taco he was eating.

"I want a fried pickle and a giant gordita." Sebastian's eyes were wide as he took in all the options surrounding them. "Look! Churros!"

"It's still early, guys. Let's take it slow, or you're going to be sick."

Bridges offered her a plate of funnel cake.

Her taste buds exploded in expectation. "You're so bad."

"Or really good at remembering your favorite." He winked. "Come on, it's not a Summerfest without a sugar-cinnamon-covered fried cake."

Pinching off a corner of the delicious dessert, she let it melt in her mouth. She might've moaned. "I don't re-member the last time I ate one of these."

"Last time I remember you eating one, you stole mine. We had just graduated from high school. It was the final summer we were here together in Port Del Mar. You stole Eduardo's too."

They walked through the food trucks, then made their way under the tents that shaded the craft dealers. The edge of the boardwalk was where the carnival began.

He bought enough tickets to play several games and a few of the rides he said he trusted. Everything was so perfect. Why was he torturing her like this?

Giving her a beautiful glimpse of what they could be as a family? Was that his plan? To give her these memories so that when he left, she saw only him? Why did she have to love him so much? This was only making his leaving worse.

After the Ferris wheel, Sebastian grabbed Cooper's hand. "There's our maze. You said we were saving it for last. Is it last? Can we go see it now?"

Bridges swallowed hard and took a deep breath. "Yes. Let's go to the maze." He wiped his hands on his jeans, like he was nervous.

The boys hollered and ran. "Look at the line." Sebastian pointed.

Cooper looked over his shoulder at them. "People like our maze."

With a wooden nod, Bridges returned a very stiff smile.

"Are you okay?" She peered at him. "What's wrong?"

He shook his head. "Nothing. This has been such a great day. I hate to see it end." He took her hand and entwined his fingers with hers. "Let's go get lost together."

Tilting her head, she studied him. But before she could ask another question, Selena De La Rosa joined them. "Hello. How's Summerfest treating you?"

The boys were so excited they were talking over each

other. Selena laughed. "Since you are the designers of our most popular maze, how would you like to stand in the crow's nest and watch over the participants?"

"Yes!" Sebastian yelled.

Cooper turned to Sebastian. "Can we, Dad?"

A warm ball of love and goo formed at her core and in her heart. She turned toward the carnival and blinked back the tears that wanted to fall. Bridges was Cooper's dad. How could he leave them?

Bridges squeezed her hand. The boys followed Selena around to the back of the maze.

He cleared his throat. "No crying in public."

"I can cry if I want."

"I was talking about me." He grinned at her. "I never realized the power one word could have."

"I know, right?" She leaned into his arm. "Is that the first time he's called you dad?"

"It was the first time it came out so naturally. Without any thought."

"Oh, Bridges." She couldn't bear to ask if that meant he was taking Cooper to Oklahoma with him. Of course, it did. She would be losing both of them.

This moment was for the boys. She funneled all her attention to their happiness. This was a big day for them. Looking up, she saw Cooper and Sebastian in the stand that overlooked the maze. They waved at her, and she took their picture.

Bridges counted the tickets out and handed them to the gatekeeper, then he took Lilianna by the hand and entered the maze.

With the first turn to the right, she laughed. "I don't think this is fair—we've seen the diagrams."

"You're right." He tapped his chin and pulled a bandanna out of his pocket.

She didn't like the mischievous glint in his eyes. "What are you doing with that?"

"I'm going to blindfold you, turn you around and walk a little way in, and then you are gonna have to get us out of here."

"Did the boys put you up to this?" She glanced up. Yep, those two were in on this.

"Come on, this is gonna be fun. I want you to know that I trust you and I'd follow you anywhere, even if you aren't sure it's the right direction."

Her muscles froze. "Bridges. What are you saying?" Was she just hearing what she wanted to hear, or was he telling her that he was staying in Port Del Mar? With her?

He stood behind her. "Can I blindfold you?"

Her mouth had forgotten how to form words, so she nodded. He blindfolded her, and her world went black. Bridges rested his hand on her shoulder. "Let's get this adventure started."

Hand out, she took a step. He was right with her, following every path she led them down. A few times, she ended up in a corner, but then a couple of helpers above them would shout out left or right.

Bridges laughed. "That's cheating."

"No, it's not. It's using the resources you have."

Still feeling her way, she came to another opening, but she couldn't find a wall.

"You did it. You led us home," he whispered in her ear as he took off the mask. She blinked in the bright sun. The boys cheered from above. Port Del Mar hummed with excitement all around her. Then she saw clusters of the most beautiful potted hydrangeas: blue, purple and pink.

Her mind was a whirl of words and thoughts. "Home?"

"I'm staying." Bridges had his arm around her. He pulled her closer and gave her a brief kiss. His lips brushed across hers. Light but solid. She leaned in for more, but he stepped back. "I took the job for a couple of reasons. One, I want Cooper to grow up with family. Two, I love you and don't want to waste any more time thinking about what I should do when I know without a doubt what I want to do."

He waved to the plants. "These are yours. For the house. I bought enough for the front and backyard. You'll be able to see them from every window. Did you know that there's a meaning for each color?"

She shook her head as she walked over to the large potted plants.

"Pink is for heartfelt emotion. I know I'm not good at emotions, but I promise to get better. Purple is for a deep desire to understand someone. And blue. Your favorite is for an apology. I'm so sorry for any hurt I've caused you."

His hand went from her neck, down her arm to her hand. "Selena is taking the boys to my mom. She's at the bakery."

He led her through the carnival to the boardwalk. He took the steps down to the beach and kept walking until they were under the pier. The water hit against the columns.

Her heart was beating so hard that her whole body was vibrating.

"I've been waiting for the right time to talk to you."

He licked his lips, then looked at the water creeping close to their feet. Standing still was becoming difficult.

"Bridges, if you don't start talking, I'm going to scream. What do you want to say?"

He rubbed his hands up and down his arms like he was cold. His breaths were shallow and rapid. She took his hands in hers and held them still. "Bridges. Look at me."

He did, then he took a deep breath. "I love you."

"I know." She cupped his face. "Are you allowing me to love you?"

"You were Eduardo's for so long. I couldn't—"

Stepping back, she let him go. "Are you still using Eduardo as an excuse not to love me? He is not the one between us right now." Her heart was going to shatter if he kept doing this.

He reached for her and pulled her back into his arms. "That came out wrong. What I'm trying to say is that I love you, and I want to have a life with you loving me."

She grabbed his face and kissed him.

He laughed between kisses. He held her so that they were staring into each other's eyes. "I'm staying in Port Del Mar because I can't imagine my life without you. I hope I haven't messed it all up. You said you wanted more. I have so much more to give you, if you still want me."

She leaned in closer and pressed her lips to his. Her arms were around his neck as his hands grasped her waist to steady her.

Breaking the kiss, she rested her forehead on his shoulder. "You're horrible. Why did you make me wait so long?"

"I didn't know if we were still on the same page, and

I didn't want to ruin the boys' big day if you'd stopped wanting more from me. I'm not easy to love."

"Oh, Bridges. That's not true."

"It is. But I want to be better. I told my mom about the secret my dad made me keep. I don't want to live with any secrets. Every moment we have together makes us stronger. I love you so much that I was afraid of losing you. I'm giving that fear to God."

Her body felt so light. "I love you, Bridges Espinoza. I'm wholly and completely yours. Are you ready for our next adventure?"

"I'll go anywhere you go."

Epilogue

The bonfire on the beach flared as his brother added a few more tall logs. The sun was low as twilight softened the sky. Fall was Bridges's favorite time on the beach. His family was throwing a party for Cooper. This morning, the judge had made everything official. Cooper was an Espinoza. His whole family and Lilianna had been there.

Reno jogged over to him. "Hey, Dad. How are you feeling? Are you going to do it tonight?"

He nodded and checked to make sure the ring his mother had given him was still there. "Cooper is mine, and now I hope Lilianna agrees to make our relationship legally binding too."

"Ouch." His brother made a face. "You're not going to say it like that, are you? She might have to say no on principle alone."

Despite the coolness of the sea air, he broke into a sweat. "What if I do this wrong and she refuses?" He scanned the beach. His brother-in-law had a grill going on his tailgate. The kids were playing a game of Frisbee. All of his sisters but Marguerite were sitting around the fire, talking and laughing. A table with drinks and snacks was set up behind them. "Is she here yet? I don't see her."

"Calm down. She's with Mom and Marguerite. They're bringing Cooper's cake and other goodies from the bakery. Brother, I don't think you can mess this up."

Cooper and Sebastian left the game and ran over to him. "Can we talk to you?"

"I've got to go check on the burgers." Reno gave Cooper a pat on the back. "Welcome to the family, *mijo.*"

The boys pulled Bridges farther from the group. "We've been doing extra chores for Abuelita and Tía Marguerite. With the money, we bought this." Cooper pulled a box out of his hoodie. "It's for Lilianna. We want you to give it to her."

Inside the little box was a silver charm of a German shepherd. "She has the one Dad gave her of the bull." He looked at Cooper.

The older brother nodded. "We thought she should have one from you too. It's like Big Mack. But it's you too. The German shepherd is fierce, loyal and always protects those they love. They're smart. She needs to know you love her so we can be a real family in one house."

Bridges lowered his head and ran a finger over the shiny charm. For a moment, he fought back the tears, but then he stopped fighting and let them go. He pulled the boys into a tight hug.

"Hey! There're my guys. Why are y'all hiding over here away from everyone?"

The boys looked at him with panic. He smiled and

patted their shoulders, but his heart jumped in triple time. She was here. "We were talking about you."

"Me? Uh-oh. What's wrong?"

Do it now, everything inside him screamed. Soon they would be in the middle of his family, and he didn't want to ask her there. They'd tell him how he should proceed. Right here was perfect. Just the four of them. His family.

He took her hand and pulled her closer to them. He took a deep breath. Was he still crying?

"Lilianna."

"Yes? Are you okay? You need to breathe."

"I love you. I love you so much I can't hold it in. I'm a mess." With the boys on either side of him, he dropped to one knee.

"Bridges?"

Taking the ring out, he held it up and offered it to her. "Lilianna, we've been best friends since we were seven. You've held my heart this whole time. Will you be my wife and hold my hand?"

She stared at the ring, then at him. Blinking.

"Mom," Sebastian whispered. "This is when you say yes."

She looked at Sebastian and then at Cooper, the tears flowing.

Bridges cleared his throat. "Just to be clear, I don't come alone. You get Cooper too."

She laughed, then covered her mouth. "Then it has to be a yes."

The boys cheered as Bridges swept her into his arms and spun.

Sebastian clapped. "I told him to spin you. Like in the movies you like."

Cooper wiped at his face, then turned his back to them. Sebastian, who was much shorter, reached up to put his arm around his older brother's shoulders. "It's okay to cry. I've seen my dad cry sometimes in videos when he'd talk to me."

Cooper looked to Bridges for confirmation. Bridges nodded. "It's true."

Lilianna had her arm around Bridges like she was never going to let go. He liked it. She cupped Cooper's face. "Eduardo cried when he was happy, excited or sad. Today, we have happy tears, right?"

He let his own tears fall. Pulling Cooper and Sebastian close, they had their first official family hug. He took a deep breath. "I love you guys." He was going to say it as often as he could. These were his boys and they were both a part of Eduardo. And now he belonged to Lilianna.

"We'd better join the party. They're being polite, but it won't last long."

The boys ran ahead, excited to share the news first.

He took Lilianna's hand and stopped her.

"What?"

"I have one more thing to do before we join the chaos." He took the trinket the boys had presented him and slipped it on to the loop with the bull charm. "The boys wanted me to give this to you to wear with Eduardo's gift."

"Thank you for not letting me throw the bracelet into the ocean when I was angry." Her eyes watered as she caressed the new charm. "It's perfect and it's so you. I love you."

He lifted her chin and pressed his lips against her soft mouth. *"Tú eres mi corazón."*

She had always been his heart, and now he was hers too.

* * * * *

If you enjoyed this story, look for these other books by Jolene Navarro:

The Texan's Secret Daughter
The Texan's Surprise Return
The Texan's Promise
The Texan's Unexpected Holiday

Dear Reader,

Thank you for visiting Port Del Mar with me. I love the idea that through these pages we get to walk together in a town created in my heart. Thank you for letting me introduce you to some of my favorite people.

The inspiration for Bridges came from collaborating with the K-9 officers at the high school where I work and an old classmate of my husband's, Ron Vasquez. He was a K-9 officer in Oklahoma. I appreciate the time he took to talk to me and the pictures he shared of his four-legged partner.

There are so many heroes in our daily lives, such as nurses and spouses of those in our military. This is where the strength of Lilianna came from. I loved giving these two a happy ending by finding the truth that God offers during the good and the trying times.

I look forward to seeing you again in the next Port Del Mar story in May. Officer Sanchez is about to get the surprise of his life. You can find me on Facebook at Jolene Navarro, author.

Jolene Navarro

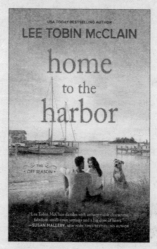